THE CALL-OUT

THE CALL-OUT

a novel in rhyme

CAT FITZPATRICK

Seven Stories Press
NEW YORK • OAKLAND • LONDON

Seven Stories Press
140 Watts Street
New York, NY 10013
www.sevenstories.com

College professors and high school and middle school teachers may order free examination copies of Seven Stories Press titles. Visit https://www.sevenstories.com/pg/resources-academics or email academics@sevenstories.com.

Library of Congress Cataloging-in-Publication Data

Names: Fitzpatrick, Cat, author.
Title: The call-out : a novel / by Cat Fitzpatrick.
Description: New York : Seven Stories Press, [2022]
Identifiers: LCCN 2022015012 | ISBN 9781644212332 (trade paperback) | ISBN 9781644212349 (ebook)
Subjects: LCGFT: Novels in verse.
Classification: LCC PS3606.I88483 C35 2022 | DDC 813/.6--dc23/eng/20220603
LC record available at https://lccn.loc.gov/2022015012

Printed in the United States of America.

9 8 7 6 5 4 3 2 1

to the trans girls of New York

When I see two trans girls in a relationship I want to ask them "which one of you is the alien and which one of you is the predator?"

—KATE FRIGGLE

contents

a year begins, with some flirtation 11

awkward moments in the morning light 23

some issues with accommodation 35

excursions into the life of the night 47

al fresco enjoyments in clement weather 59

an annual community get-together 71

transsexual literature takes the stage 83

a disco full of lust and rage 95

everyone deals with consequences 107

complications of a daytime date 119

on taking control of one's own fate 131

a discussion regarding various offenses 143

some episodes of lateral strife 155

another year, another life? 167

epilogue: top-voted comment 181

acknowledgments 185

Posted 2nd February by @Eunuch_Onegin in series The Call-Out
creator chose not to give content warnings
tags: inspired by poetry; trans; transition

a year begins,
with some flirtation
(1/14)

New Year. Of course, I went out drinking.
Everyone knows that I'm a lush:
talk is much jollier than thinking,
you're never so light as in a crush.
A friend of mine had a shift bartending,
stirring up negronis and hand-blending
frozen margaritas like a pro,
and everyone who was in the know
had come to drink her potent potions.
The bar was full, the bar was loud
(what else would you expect from a crowd
with testo voices, but estro emotions?),
"sexy mean" and "kinky dork,"
half the damn trans girls in New York.

Probably somewhere someone was crying
or fighting, but as far as I could see
flirtatious chatter and lustful spying
was the dominant activity.
Look, for instance, with what evident meaning
that girl in denim, awkwardly leaning
against the wall, flicks her eyes across
at that one with hair like candy floss.
Pink Hair peeks back, then drains her libation,
pulls out her fags, slides off her chair
and leaves the bar, tossing her hair.
Denim, with a shake of determination,
as if dismissing a lingering doubt
crosses the room, and follows her out.

Intentions, however, need application
and Denim (alright, her name is Day)
instead gets stuck in hesitation
as she exits through the entranceway.
How do you cope if you get a rejection?
And facing a girl of such femme perfection,
how do you avoid being cast as the bloke?
But now, she's outside, without a smoke,
or much in the way of warm attire,
in a New York winter, in the freezing air,
and she's freezing up. But then Pink Hair
(sensing her plight? Or from desire?)
turns, and says —"Hi, I'm Bette.
Perhaps you'd like a cigarette?"

From there things quickly get more flirty;
they find each other on the internet
and check their mutuals (they have like, thirty)
Bette wonders how they've never met;
they're both like three years post-transition
share musical taste and political position . . .
Day explains that although she's been
a girl for a while, she's new to the scene:
—"I used to be really depressed and quiet
stayed home, didn't eat, smoked way too much weed!
But not anymore! I realized what I need
is to go to the gym instead of diet
and, um, that Cialis is a better drug . . ."
She gives a grin and then a shrug.

Bette understands the implication.
She smiles back —"Oh, is that true?
I hear it aids the, um, circulation?"
Pauses. "Hey, I love your tattoo!"
A classic gambit. She is alluding
to where on Day's wrist, pointedly protruding
below her cuff, a "T4T"
is rendered, amateurishly.
—"That? That's nothing!" Day laughs. It's colder
than weather should be, but she's keen to impress
this girl, and so she proceeds to undress,
baring an image on her shoulder
of fallopian tubes attached to a pentacle,
and unzipping her jeans to reveal a tentacle.

Although they're only newly acquainted
Bette seems unfazed by these displays.
—"Wow, they're pretty. It's like they're painted!"
She bends to inspect, and there she stays
allowing the heat of her breath to linger
for a second, before extending a finger,
then stopping, and asking, "um . . . can I touch?"
And that's enough! Or else too much.
I'm of an older generation,
I've learnt what sex can put at stake
for us; I don't know what to make
of all these kids and their liberation.
I know they're blithe and fresh and free,
but it's all a bit too much for me.

What am I doing in this vision?
I never expected to end up here.
I grew up surrounded by derision,
everyone rejected me, straight or queer.
And now I'm thirty-something, I'm single,
I'm drinking whilst these youngsters mingle.
Perhaps I'm jealous, even obsessed;
I'm also worried. We're second-best
(here I pause to down my whisky)
even to other "girls like us."
If you're trans, the truth is thus:
even dreaming of love is risky.
I watch through the window with growing dismay.
I don't try to warn them, but I can't look away.

Well maybe it's true that I'm old and bitter,
but I was a witness. And I want to say
something about it. I deleted my Twitter
(whenever I checked it, it ruined my day)
so instead, in a fit of desperation
I'm posting this extended narration,
and (to make it even worse)
I'm going to tell the story in verse.
Some of what happened I picked up after,
and some of it I overheard,
and sometimes I've guessed at what occurred.
Is this story tragic? Or fit for laughter?
Do we ever learn from the things we do?
Sweethearts, god, I wish I knew.

But back to that night! I realized I needed
really quite sharply to visit the loo
(spiro's demands cannot go unheeded)
but when I get there, of course there's a queue!
As I wait I talk to the girl behind me.
We've met at a picnic (she has to remind me)
way back in the season the Yanks call "fall."
So many new faces! How can I recall?
Especially when everyone constantly switches
their names around, from Luna to Flick
to Corvid (why is it that trans women pick
the names of spies, goddesses, bitches,
whereas all the trans guys seem to take
sweet little names, like Josh or Jake?)

So, this girl says her name is Gaia.
She's twenty-three, uses "she" and "her,"
and works at a well-known sex toy supplier
paying off the debt she had to incur
in order to study classics in college.
She quickly imparts all of this knowledge
(her gestures are campy, her diction is fleet;
her eyes throughout stay trained on my feet)
but then descends into awkward silence,
so I ask about the connection of Latin with sex.
She's off again —"Well, that's complex!
Like, Romans have this obsession with violence,
like, for Ovid sex is basically rape,
which is why all those women have to change their shape,

and yes, I'm turned on by transformation,
who isn't? But if you know he used to hit
his girlfriend, it's a different situation.
And even Petronius, who's gay as shit,
my favorite Roman, has a kid defiled
in an orgy scene. A literal child!
There's even blood! Of course I adore
his shamelessness, but I can't ignore
abuse. Perhaps it's anachronistic
to expect Romans to seek consent . . .
I identify as being decadent,
kinky, and sado-masochistic,
but I think the more you want to screw
the more ethical work you have to do.

"Romans care more about what's fitting
than morality, their main concern
is who has power and who's submitting
and is it you? But we have to learn
that even in play you can easily be triggered . . ."
Don't the young ones have it all figured
out, I think —". . . or silenced or just
stop consenting. Being caught up in lust
doesn't mean abuse isn't being committed.
Consent is important. I volunteer
as a Dungeon Monitor at this queer
kinky orgy. No cis men admitted.
Oh hey!" And now she looks at me,
"You should come. I'll get you in for free."

I blink and flush with consternation.
Is this, I wonder, how millennials woo?
What is the meaning of this invitation?
How can I refuse? And then the loo
opens. I flee, leaving behind me
a brief excuse —"I'm on Facebook, come find me!"
I feel bad. I don't mean to be rude.
When I come out she's engrossed in some dude.
I smile, wave, and keep on walking,
then turn to see I've walked right by
a friend, name of Kate. I don't say hi:
she and her girlfriend Aashvi are talking.
However, since I'm sitting near
I cannot help but overhear.

Aashvi begins —"Are we going to do it?
It's a good time to start. Your New Year."
—"I don't know how I'll get through it.
I mean, I want this. But there's also this fear,
or something else, maybe sorrow,
I mean, it's a lot." —"We'll start tomorrow.
We'll do this together, I'll be there.
Come on, now smile. Do not despair."
—"Well, I suppose no one ever gave a
promise creation had to be nice:
of course there's got to be sacrifice."
—"Such gloom! You almost sound like Kristeva."
What? I find myself wanting to shout!
What is it that they're talking about?

—"Well, whatever, I love Kristeva.
She's my problematic fave."
— "Oh dear, you're such a second-waver."
—"Kristeva's too French to be second-wave."
—"She's racist enough!" —"If I'm stopping taking
hormones to make my body start making
sperm again, then I'm going to need
feminist theories of motherhood to read."
My stomach twists. My mind races.
My God, I think, they're planning a child!
She's going off hormones! That's fucking wild!
Will it work? I've heard of cases,
friends of friends, on the internet
but never a person I've actually met.

The doctors told me that the very second
you so much as ask for estrogen
you immediately stop being fecund,
and never ever become so again.
But that's the doctors, they can't be trusted:
if they think of us breeding, they're disgusted.
They want us sterile. So possibly, maybe,
if she goes off hormones Kate'll have a baby!
And more importantly, be a mother!
I see her with a child of her own to hold
and surrounded by family when she's old:
I don't think I've been so jealous of another
woman, ever. Even when my cis
friends got pregnant, it wasn't like this.

Well, I try to conceal my agitation
and—let's be honest—down half my drink,
while they continue their conversation:
—"My dear! The feminists will clearly all think
motherhood is simply patriarchal coercion
and secretly wish to develop some version
of compulsory collective childcare."
—"Well, that, or else they'll believe that they're
naturally nurturing . . ." —"But nature is real!
I naturally desire a child of my own."
—"Me too! And I hate testosterone.
Is that natural too? I don't want to feel . . .
Ugh, it's horrific! If theory's no good,
are there horror films about motherhood?

The People Under the Stairs maybe,
or *The Babadook*, or *The Exorcist*,
or that lesbian remake of *Rosemary's Baby*?
I bet I could sell BuzzFeed a list:
"Horror Movies For When You're Expecting."
People play Mozart in the hopes of affecting
unborn children, well, same idea:
teach the fetus how to fear.
As soon as you're pregnant we're watching *It Follows*!"
—"As soon as, you say? That suggests that we'll try . . ."
—"I guess . . ." Kate gives a theatrical sigh.
I finish my beer in two more swallows.
Day and Bette are coming back in.
I don't know which has a dopier grin.

—"So," Day says, "what can I get you?"
—"Oh, I got it. I'll pay my own check."
—"But I can afford it!" —"Okay, then I'll let you
buy me a bourbon. You must be in tech!"
—"I measure risk for corporations
to help them plan their operations."
—"Capitalism is so absurd."
—"Well I've always been kind of a nerd,
and I'm good at worrying." —"Of course you are, honey."
—"I did an actuarial science degree.
It actually rewards your anxiety,
and there's lots of jobs, and it pays good money.
Though now I'm trans they all think I'm insane.
Are you sure just whisky? We could have champagne . . ."

I get out of my seat. I'm thinking of ghosting.
Gaia's talking to this girl by the door,
Keiko, maybe? Gaia is boasting
about her makeup: —"I splurged on Dior.
It's just the reddest! And I put foundation
on my lips before the application
to increase the contrast." —"Oh my gosh, you know
so many cool tricks." —"If you want I can show
them all to you: contouring, blending . . ."
—"I'd love to learn to do makeup right."
—"Oh wow, hey look, it's almost midnight.
You wanna make out while the year is ending?"
Midnight! Already! Keiko starts to blush,
and I head to the bar to beat the rush.

Fuck, it's New Year, the time of new chances.
The clock goes dong, someone starts to sing
"Auld Lang Syne," and everyone dances.
Tonight we dream that everything
that makes our lives such a shambles
could maybe be changed. This year our gambles
if we're daring, and have discipline,
might pay off. I take us in
over a fresh whisky sour
and want to burst into tears.
These messy, broke, lonely queers!
Here we all are, seizing the hour
in this great, relentless metropolis:
me, and three couples, each locked in a kiss.

Posted 12th March by @Eunuch_Onegin in series The Call-Out
creator chose not to give content warnings
tags: art; communal housing; Bach

awkward moments in the morning light
(2/14)

I'm guessing that night was full of caresses
and meaningful convos, but now it's done,
and the aftermath of its excesses
is risen upon by the wintry sun.
The city always seems enchanting
mornings like these, the light slanting
between the buildings, and reaching deep
into the bedrooms, to wake you from sleep.
Day opens her eyes to a strange ceiling
and sits bolt upright, then remembers, she met
that girl . . . She turns and looks at Bette,
who's deep asleep. Day grins and, feeling
horny, she kisses Bette's neck for a bit
then runs her fingers down to Bette's clit.

Bette turns. —"Oomph. What are you doing?"
Day freezes. Bette smiles, sleepily:
—"S'okay, it's nice. T4T.
Give me some of that next-day wooing."
And now let's skip ahead an hour
or two: they've fucked, and had a shower,
(where they fucked again) and picked their way
through the kitchen, which is in disarray:
it smells, the floor is sticky as toffee
and the sink is clogged with unwashed plates—
Bette blames it all on her many roommates—
to retreat with their prizes (a pot of coffee,
some Jif, some jam, and some Wonder Bread)
to the safety of Bette's single bed.

(Regarding Bette's flat, a brief divagation:
it's a walk-up in Brooklyn, well south of the park,
above a launderette with a bad reputation.
Four windows, eight rooms: the whole place is dark;
the rooms are tiny, the partitions are flimsy,
the paint is peeling. There are touches of whimsy,
a large stuffed goat with a Stalin pin,
a struggling fern in an old soup tin,
an artistically defaced Bikini Kill poster,
but what you notice first are the messes.
There are piles of clothing, lamé dresses
and latex shorts, it seems like most of
the contents of the local thrift store
have been requisitioned, then dumped on the floor.

There's a purple dildo in the shower
and elsewhere in the bathroom, several more.
There are three switchblades in the cutlery drawer
but only one fork. There's a sort of tower
of mysterious amps, laptops, and cable
taking up half of the only table.
No-one has ever cleaned anything at all.
It's sort of like Eden right after The Fall
before Eve had figured how to deal
with the sudden freedom of being cast
out into the world, so beautiful and vast
and cold, and ineluctable, and real.)
Bette gives Day a kiss, tells her she's gay
and makes them both sandwiches with PB&J.

Day munches, then giggles. —"I feel like a child!"
—"I only eat these," Bette says, "and pills."
She gestures to her nightstand, which is piled
with orange and green prescription refills.
"And ramen, as well. Though not in that order."
—"You're a pharmaceutical hoarder!"
—"Your pleasure is something you have to pursue.
I know what I like. What about you?"
—"I dunno. I mean, it's been nice to meet you.
Um. I have a Nintendo Switch.
I just got *Smash Bros.*" —"Oh my God, you bitch,
invite me over, I will totally whip you
if I play as Samus." —"Well, it's not far.
Wanna go now? I can call a car."

And so, Bette brings a pair of knickers,
some noodles, and some Percocets
and gets Day to stop the cab for liquors
(Maker's and Cocchi) and cigarettes
(Spirits). Her instructions are emphatic:
—"Drinking bad liquor is problematic!"
Day laughs, wide eyes: she's absorbing it all.
Her building's the kind with an entrance hall,
pre-war, when apartments used to be bigger:
she lives in two whole rooms alone,
though the only things she seems to own
are a TV, some boxes, and a Gundam figure.
Bette gapes at all the empty space
in disbelief —"Wow. Nice place."

And here I'll leave these two to honey
(though we'll miss the bit where Bette ascertains
Day has no saucepans. That bit is funny)
and refocus on Bushwick, a room that contains
Gaia and Keiko. Is barely containing,
I should say, since Gaia is nervously obtaining
her garments, scattered here and there,
(she can't find her bra, which is under a chair)
in preparation for splitting while Keiko slumbers.
The search isn't easy: the room, though small,
has art supplies from wall to wall,
and those walls are pinned with significant numbers
of exquisite landscapes, whose details include
much both meticulous and rude.

These, once noticed, are quite beguiling:
Forgetting her bra, Gaia stands in her jeans
hunting for the pairs of tall girls defiling
each other in these classic sylvan scenes.
And not just couples: sometimes they're poly!
It's like a sexy bucolic *Where's Wally?*
if the artist had come to it by way
of serious study of *ukiyo-e*.
She's so charmed by one combination—
two tiny girls are restraining a third
in a forest clearing, watched by a bird—
that she makes a joyful exclamation.
It's loud enough that Keiko wakes,
and groans: —"Oooh, my head, it aches."

Gaia jumps —"Oh sorry, I'd forgotten
that you were there. Your art is, like,
really interesting. Like a misbegotten
child of Hiroshige who's a hot trans dyke.
It's so cool how you take this tradition
and give it contemporary rendition,
but it's also timeless, like a fantasy."
—"Oh yeah, that's Greenwood Cemetery."
Keiko looks bleary and disconcerted.
"It's the view from just inside the gate.
They're all in New York, or New York State.
See the mausoleums? I've just inserted
the people." —"Oh right! Like what if these places,
we're told are public, were actual safe spaces?

That's clever! A contemporary re-engineering
of something like the Hundred Famous Views
depicting these sites, but also queering
their function by implanting the bodies they refuse."
—"Um, I mean, Hiroshige's decent,
but my favorite stuff is a bit more recent,
Yoshida Hiroshi is, like, the best.
But . . . how come you're getting dressed?
Were you . . . ghosting? That's kind of scuzzy."
—"Oh. Well, um." Gaia stares at her feet.
"My memories of last night are . . . incomplete,
like, did we have sex? It's sort of fuzzy.
And when you don't know that it's awkward to stay
for breakfast. What are you supposed to say?

"Ugh, I'm sorry. I've been enacting
a terrible model of consent to sex.
What I should have been doing is interacting
to process what each of us recollects . . ."
—"We didn't have sex, you can stop freaking
out about it. We were too busy speaking!
We were drunk. It was fun. We did these weird shots,
you said they were 'picklebacks' . . . I think we did lots,
and you taught me this game where after drinking
we'd slap each other. One time you missed.
I think you were drunk. And also we kissed."
—"Whisky Slaps? What was I thinking?
And I just remembered I tried to show
you how to do makeup. You're an artist! You know!"

—"But I've only been a girl since September,
I don't know those tricks. I think they're cool."
—"Oh god, what else am I going to remember?
Why do I always act like a fool?
Fuck, I've got to try to be calmer,
even now I'm bringing the drama!
Sorry. Listen, you seem really sweet . . ."
—"Yeah, I had fun. Perhaps we can meet
again?" —"Yeah maybe, when I'm not in a panic.
Why can't I find my bra anywhere?"
—"Don't worry, it's just beneath that chair."
—"Your art is great! Sorry I'm manic!"
And just like that she's up and flown,
and Keiko is sitting in the bed, alone.

Meanwhile, in another part of the city
(to be precise, the Lower East Side),
Kate is also feeling shitty.
She wants to sleep but she's been wide
awake for ages. Aashvi is snoring.
She could ignore that, but there's no ignoring
the jostling thoughts inside her head.
Eventually she gets out of bed.
Normally on the first she'd do her injection,
regular as a period. She glances down
at her body, picks a dressing gown
from off the floor, sighs with dejection,
and pads into the other room
hoping some coffee will cut through her gloom.

It's cold, but it's bright. It isn't snowing.
It's one of those days when it's going to snow.
It's one of those days when you're almost knowing
something you somehow still don't know.
The weather's changing. It's all potential.
There's a steep pressure differential:
it's about to drop, low and fast.
Something's changing. This just can't last.
Kate makes a coffee, gets out a skinny
Vogue cigarette, and opens wide
the window, letting the cold inside.
The breeze has a taste, it's sour and tinny.
She stares at the sky as if she's about
to grab the frame and fling herself out.

Behind her she hears the parquet creaking
—"Good morning doll-face, want some ca-fay?"
This is Aashvi's joke: she loves speaking
in a highly unconvincing "American way."
(Her years in New York have failed at diluting,
one bit, her cultivated, high-faluting
Indian accent.) Kate flicks her butt
out of the window and pulls it shut.
Aashvi steps closer and gives her a nuzzle.
"Kiss me, sweetness," Kate turns her head.
—"I'm sad. Wanna watch a movie in bed,"
she asks, "and make out and maybe guzzle
unhealthy snacks?" —"Well first I should
complete a few tasks, or else I would."

—"But it's New Year's Day!" —"And I've been intending
to repaint the skirting, and work on that grant,
and collate my expenses: there are taxes pending."
—"Oh Aashvi, it's January!" —"But by April I can't
remember them all." —"You're so efficient,
you make me feel like I'm deficient."
Aashvi laughs. —"Oh my suffering sweet!
Why don't I make you something to eat?"
—"Do you think we could make an approximation
of Israeli eggs? Like, Israeli-ish?"
—"It's called Shakshouka. It's an Arabic dish!
This is also part of the occupation
of Palestine—both culture and land!
But yes, I can make that. Come, give me a hand."

They kiss again, then start cooking.
One peels and chops, one spices and salts.
They step past each other without looking
or seeming to try, a culinary waltz,
set to the carefully eclectic curation
of tunes on an internet radio station.
They step and turn and pirouette
around the floor of their kitchenette.
Aashvi fries up garlic in oil,
and Kate chops tomatoes coarse
then gives them to Aashvi to make into sauce
and when the sauce reaches a boil
they break in the eggs, turn down the heat,
warm some pita, and sit down to eat.

Lulled by this domestic rhythm
Kate's headache and nausea fade away
and most of her sadness goes with them,
or perhaps she just forgets to pay
attention to it, the food's so delicious,
and then they have to wash the dishes,
and so, when Aashvi gets out the paint
she barely makes a cursory complaint
("Why can't you be more of a procrastinator?")
before sighing loudly, kneeling down,
getting a brush, and going to town
on the baseboards. And when, some two hours later,
they're finally painted "Snowflake White,"
she gets out her laptop and starts to write!

So much for Kate and her useful labors.
As for me, I'm pulled from a pleasant dream
about trains at like eight by my bloody neighbor's
child practicing the Star Wars theme
again. Then again. I pull the cover
over my ears. If you don't have a lover
then the world ought to compensate
by letting you at least sleep in late.
I fucking hate mornings. And living in a city.
And the straight family that lives next door.
And my stupid brain that can't ignore
some child mistreating a famous ditty.
Is it any wonder I'm depressed?
All I want is to get some rest.

I've often thought, if the world was my oyster
and I could somehow escape this snare
I call my life, I'd live in a cloister
alone, up on a cliff somewhere
near the sea, so I could hear the beating
of waves on the rocks, and walk without meeting
a soul. Instead, what's available to me
is my morning cup of green tea.
I groan, get up and heat the kettle
to seventy-seven degrees, and choose
a Yellow Mountain, and while it brews
I put on some Bach. And then I can settle
down for a while, all curled up,
in my favorite chair, with my favorite cup.

I try to let go of my vexation
and put myself in a state of calm.
The choir is singing Luther's translation
of the one hundred and thirtieth psalm.
"Ob bei uns ist der sünden viel"
their voices tell me, and I almost feel
comforted. The tea is such pure green,
so vegetal, so sharp, so clean.
It smells like life, like hay and flowers.
At the bitter turning of the year
it promises spring is drawing near.
The day's ahead, full of hours.
I drink the tea. The cantata plays.
The year's ahead, full of days.

Posted 7th April by @Eunuch_Onegin in series The Call-Out
content warnings: love
tags: pizza; education; coition

some issues with accommodation

(3/14)

A few months later, spring is springing:
the hard dead ground has gone all soft;
daffs and hyacinths are flinging
the limbs of their green new bodies aloft,
to catch the photons that induce vibration
in certain electrons in their pigmentation,
and waving their genitals in the breeze,
bright and fragrant, to attract the bees;
They're not the only ones enjoying the weather
or feeling sexy. Bette and Day
are sitting al fresco at a hipster café,
making out and giggling together.
From the next table, some bro-dudes stare
but neither of the girls appears to care.

They look like they know that they look fantastic.
For Bette, that's standard. The girl has dash.
Her sunglasses are large, turquoise and plastic,
her tight red dress and her pink hair clash
precisely. But Day's been glowing up.
Sitting there cradling her cardboard cup,
she's disheveled but poised. She's wearing this
top with the slogan "0% Cis,"
cropped at the waist, and a velvet choker;
her shorts are short, and so is her hair;
she wears grey lipstick, and sports a pair
of stripy stockings. She sips her mocha
(Bette has espresso) strokes Bette's cheek,
and makes a small noise like she's trying to speak.

—"What?" Bette asks. —"I think I love you"
—"You're such a girl! Oh my God."
—"No but I do." —"Do I have to shove you
off your chair?" She gives Day a prod,
grabs her by the neck, then tries to bite her
but Day is not in the mood to fight her.
She shakes Bette off, takes her hand.
—"This isn't going how I planned . . ."
She pauses. "You know you're always staying
over? I wondered, do you think you'd like . . ."
—"You want to U-Haul! Holy fuck, you dyke!"
—"Okay, I guess, but like, you're paying
so much in rent, it doesn't make sense . . ."
—"Stop," says Bette, "this is too intense."

She takes a deep breath. "OK, it's true that
moving in with you would save me rent,
but let's suppose I wanted to do that,
we'd need to be clear on what it meant.
You're not the only person I'm dating,
and just this morning I was masturbating
dressed as a baby online for some dude.
My job is strangers seeing me nude,
you know, I like to fuck and do molly,
I didn't transition to 'be a dyke wife',
I'm not about having a 'stable' life!
This isn't even like 'we can be poly.'
I like you, but I don't have a 'primary,'
I just have people I'm happy to see."

Day smiles broadly. How is she containing
her hurt? Doesn't this cause her pain?
—"Yeah, I get that." —"I'm just explaining . . ."
— "It's fine, I mean, you don't need to explain."
Bette smiles too. —"You mean that? Really?"
—"I do. I mean, I like you. Clearly.
I just said I loved you. I'm sorry. It's true."
—"It's okay. I, like, I like you too,
but love as a discourse is really oppressive."
—"I know. I get that. And that's totally fine.
So: do you wanna move into mine?
I promise not to be possessive."
—"If I sleep around, then I'll be afraid
you'll get resentful that you aren't getting laid."

—"Right now I'm not sure I'd be attracted
to anyone who wasn't basically your clone."
—"Oh whatever! You're just distracted
by emotions. I blame the progesterone.
Grows your titties but makes you crazy.
We'll work on your Grindr. You can't be lazy.
All these hotties everywhere
won't fuck themselves! And it's not fair
to expect me to do all the fornication.
If I'm moving in, we should share the work.
You're a functional top! I can't let you shirk
what's basically a sacred obligation.
There's a shortage of tops! Don't ration that D!"
—"Okay, yeah, fine, enough, I agree!"

By now Day has started laughing,
Bette laughs as well, then they kiss,
and one of the cis bros makes a barfing
noise. Day turns and shouts out —"Piss
the fuck back off to fucking Hoboken
or your hetero nose is gonna get broken!"
and the bro goes silent in utter shock
so then she continues, "Eat my cock!"
and cackles, as if she's the one with power,
but of course she isn't. And so they stand
and run down the street, hand in hand.
Behind them the bros just sit and glower.
When they stop at last, Bette says, —"Alright.
I'll get to looking for a sublet tonight."

The move proceeds without complication.
One of Bette's roommates has a friend
in some kind of hostile living situation
(don't they always?) and so by the end
of a fortnight, Bette has wholesale imported
her pills, her clothes, and all her assorted
impedimenta and knick-knacks. The disarray
seems to actually be pleasing to Day
and so Bette decides to call in the swapsie.
She makes a Manhattan, gets Day a beer
watches her drink it, then whispers in her ear:
—"Your Grindr has died. It's time to autopsy.
I'm sorry to have to break the news."
—"Oh Bette, do I have to? Can't I refuse?"

—"I know we're not together, precisely,
but it's too unbalanced if I'm getting sex
and you're staying home. Doesn't matter how nicely
we act to each other, there'll be bad effects.
Been there before. It makes things lopsided.
Also monogamy is just misguided."
—"OK, but I've got a confession to make.
I don't have a Grindr. I'm a big fake.
I have OkCupid, but somehow I've never
really used it. I start to compare
myself with the cis girls and just despair.
I've only had sex with like . . . eight people ever."
—"Oh, sweetheart! Of course. I should have known!
Don't worry. I'll help. Unlock your phone."

Bette downloads Grindr, sets up a profile
fills in Day's gender, position, and race,
opens the camera, and tells Day to smile,
takes a picture which doesn't include her face,
selects "right now" as her desired connection,
thinks, then writes in the "about me" section:
Hung trans top, 6 inches and thicc
if you buy me pizza you can suck my dick.
In minutes Day's messages have caught on fire
and her telephone is vibrating non-stop.
Bette's not surprised: "You're a functional top,
no strings, you're just what they all desire."
—"I don't think I can fuck a cisgender man."
—"You're great at fucking. Of course you can."

She shows her "subbyboylookin2sucU."
Day looks at his message, gives a frown, then a grin,
then types, —"oh so you want me to fuck you?"
Bette squeals: —"Yesss! Just jump right in!"
They're both all giddy. After specifying
the toppings she'd find most gratifying
Day tells the boy he's a pizza slut
who needs to enema his faggot butt.
—"This is fun," she says. "It's almost a pity
I'm not gonna actually screw this guy."
—"Oh darlin', you're just so cute when you're shy.
For sure you should screw him. Oh, you look so pretty!"
Bette sounds like a mother, preparing to send
her daughter to stay the night with a friend.

And so, just like a good little daughter
Day takes some condoms and heads out the door
and, to make a short story shorter,
she doesn't have them any more
by the time she returns. In their place she's acquired
not only the pizza she pre-required
(half-eaten) but also some zeppoli.
Bette's like —"Get those away from me,"
and Day's like —"Your loss. They taste fantastic.
That wasn't at all as creepy as I'd feared,
although I guess it was kind of weird.
This dude was so enthusiastic
about my body. He loved my dick."
—"Bet you a dollar," Bette says, "he's a chick."

—"What?" —"Most dudes who want to date us
are unhatched eggs, but with jobs or a wife
which make them too scared to imitate us
and ruin their comfortable cishet life.
But as long as you view it as a transaction
who cares why they have a 'trans-attraction'?"
—"But I have a job." —"And now you're out,
does it make it harder?" —"Well yeah. No doubt . . .
So, he was only interested
because he's secretly a tranny too?"
Bette clicks her teeth. —"In some ways that's true,
but you have to ask why you're invested
in abstract notions of attractive or not.
You just need someone to think you're hot."

—"He definitely did. It was almost pathetic."
—"And did you feel sexy as well?"
—"I mean, that head was . . . energetic.
Yeah, I guess I felt sexy as hell."
—"And did you get pizza?" —"Yes! It's delicious!
And also, unlike ramen, nutritious."
—"I have my principles. But I might enjoy
consuming you, like you consumed that boy."
And then . . . I'm sorry, it's too upsetting,
I have to stop and take a breath.
It's like I'm recounting someone's death,
then I read it over, and they're only getting
laid and laughing, and hanging out.
What am I so upset about?

So, it was spring. No wait, the present
is the tense I've chosen. Okay, resume:
it's spring. The weather continues pleasant,
the daffodils wither, the tulips bloom,
Day throws herself into online dating
and tweets about how it's liberating,
and has a threesome or two with Bette,
who starts reducing her credit card debt,
and watching docs about mountaineering
accidents. Things are going well
at least as far as one can tell
from outside, or based on what I'm hearing.
Then Day gets home one night from work
and announces: —"My boss is such a jerk."

—"What happened?" —"Okay, I went in wearing
my black tank top, 'cause it's almost hot,
which is just, like, normal, but it meant I was baring
my tattoos a bit. Okay, a lot.
And I saw this bitch from human resources,
Susan, or something, who always enforces
the regulations. Like if someone brings cake
she'll turn up to judge how much you can take.
She's like, 'Satanic symbols? Really?'
So I'm like, oh fuck, but I just played dumb.
Then my boss emails, asking me to come
into his office. So I know, like, clearly
what this is about. I go in, sit down,
he's acting awkward, has this giant frown.

"And he's like, 'I'm afraid your current clothing
isn't professional. You should wear a shirt.'
He's staring at my tattoo with this look of loathing,
but whatever, fuck normics, the thing that hurt
is he didn't say blouse. Which was calculated.
He wanted me to feel humiliated.
Half the women are in tops without sleeves,
and have tattoos of flowers, but no-one believes
I'm a girl at my work, they all think I'm a liar,
and they express that through like, microaggression.
They don't want a tranny in their 'profession'
but I'm too much trouble to actually fire!
They're such a pile of pieces of shit.
I should save them the trouble and fucking quit."

Bette strokes Day's hair. —"I'm sorry they're not better.
Microaggressions are real and bad."
—"In my mind I keep writing my resignation letter.
The more I go over it the more I get mad."
—"Darlin', I get that this fuckery is upsetting
but remember the actual salary you're getting.
If you quit this job you're fucking insane.
You're never gonna earn this much money again."
—"Well, I don't know, I mean, one solution
is I could cam like you, and go back to school."
—"Day, get a grip, don't be a fool.
You are not cut out for prostitution,
and now they've passed this SESTA law
that might not even be possible any more.

—"But say that it is, and even assuming
you get some fans, and you graduate
to exclusive shows, and business is booming,
which I don't exactly anticipate,
camming as a career is super taxing:
you're not just showing your tits and relaxing,
you have to stay hard all day long
and your Instagram game has to be strong
and half your days are still dead losses,
but the thing that really does you harm
is all the trying to please and charm
fucking dudes. I don't have bosses
but you should hear the shit my clients say
every hour of the fucking day."

—"Ok, but listen, it wouldn't be forever:
I'd get a degree in something I enjoyed."
—"Day, I'm not saying you aren't clever
but the reason you're gainfully employed
while most of us seem doomed to fail
is you got that job while you still looked male.
Employers are all cisnormative!
And if you don't have a job where will we live?
Struggling sucks. You don't want to struggle."
Day huffs, but then says, —"I know, you're right.
Maybe I could do some courses at night,
or find some other way to juggle
doing this job and planning to get out?
Oh, I don't know what I'm talking about!"

Bette scoops her up, they hug in silence
for quite a long time. Your heart just breaks.
The world is full of structural violence
quite apart from all our own mistakes,
and yet amongst this we're all still driven
to process, forgive and be forgiven,
to help each other, to listen, to relate,
and tie other humans to our stupid fate,
just like all the other stupid creatures
reaching out, now that it's spring,
the frogs that croak, the birds that sing.
I guess this is just one of the features
of being alive: you have to care
about all these people you meet everywhere.

Posted 10th May by @Eunuch_Onegin in series The Call-Out
content warnings: trans men
tags: castration; vaporwave; after dark

excursions into the
life of the night
(4/14)

Let the spring rewind: watch all the flowers
close, and their stems curl into the seed;
the May warmth chill and the April showers
rise into the clouds, the turtles recede
under the ice, to sit without doing
much at all, except accruing
acid in their shells, and watching the sun
for some indication that winter's done.
The short cold days are always distressing
for Keiko too, and so, apart
from when she has classes, she just makes art
and rereads comics. It's productive but depressing.
Then March comes along and mitigates the gloom,
and she stirs, and decides to tidy her room.

She puts her sketchbooks into piles,
arranges her pencils by depth of hue,
then starts to gather the lino tiles
she uses for printblocks. As she glances through
she comes on the one that Gaia commended.
She stares at it, hard, then, since they friended
each other at some point during that night,
she opens Messenger and starts to write.
—"Hi," she types, "it's been a while
but I'd really like to be your friend.
Can we hang out?" She adds at the end
a blushing emoji with a nervous smile.
Gaia writes back almost straight away:
—"Oh hi! I'm maybe free today?"

They go back and forth in clumsy vacillation
until finally Gaia suggests a place:
a peculiar hipster amalgamation
of bar, taxidermist, and performance space
specializing in frozen alcoholic potation.
It's down on Atlantic, in the charming location
of a rezoned oil and tire shop.
They've kept the old sign. It's called Quick Stop.
Keiko's on time, right to the minute.
She orders a slushy and gives them a look
at her sister's ID, which she secretly took.
Her drink has a plastic elephant in it.
Gaia's late. Her apologies are profuse.
Her fro-yo is garnished with a plastic moose.

Now it's necessary to make conversation.
—"I'm really sorry I was late!"
Gaia repeats. Then an inspiration:
discuss the bar! "So isn't this great?"
—"There's lots of . . . animals?" Keiko queries.
—"So many! And they have this performance series.
Tonight's Bloody Mary. They're this enby queen
who's like, the greatest thing on the scene."
—"I've never seen a drag queen performing."
—"They're one of our closest analogies
to the classical Cybeleian mysteries.
This ritualized gender non-conforming,
a licensed transgression, a traditional threat . . .
How haven't you been to a drag show yet?"

—"Cybeleian?" —"Yeah! Like, Magna Mater?
This Roman goddess with cross-dressing priests,
who had an actual imperial charter
to hold these, like, castration feasts.
They'd sever their testicles, then run off shrieking
into the fancy areas, seeking
some rich guy's house, and then they'd throw
their balls through the door, and refuse to go
until they got paid. They'd fall into trances,
and prophesy, and curse, and generally be mean.
They dyed their hair, played the tambourine,
had public sex, did wild dances . . .
They wanted to ban them, but never dared.
Even the emperors were way too scared."

—"I like this idea. We should be scary.
Like, girls don't have to be nice and polite!"
—"Well, you should stay to see Bloody Mary."
So they sit drinking slushies until ten at night,
when Mary starts singing (not lip-syncing).
They start as a rich white lady, who's been drinking
and is trying to lure her gardener to bed
with a version of "Can't Get You Out of My Head";
they do "Dancing With Myself" (by Billy Idol)
as an incel in a trench coat driving a van
into a crowd; they do "Rocket Man"
as Kim Jong-Un, getting more homicidal,
until they reveal they were Trump all along
and destroy the world at the end of the song.

I'm there too, at a different table
away in the back. I don't love the place
but Mary's worth seeing. And so I'm able
to see the expression on Keiko's face.
She's in raptures: no exaggeration.
She tries to start a standing ovation.
She stamps. She cheers. When the show is done
she turns to Gaia: —"Ohmigod that was *fun*!
I'd heard that drag was misogynistic
but that was art. Hey, you wanna make out?"
Gaia makes a face like she's struggling with doubt.
—"I usually try not to be moralistic
but you're drunk, and after the thing at New Year
I think it's not a great idea."

And that is that. The moment is shattered.
Gaia broke it. Keiko looks crushed
and Gaia gabbles, as if words mattered
in matters of the body. Their goodbyes are rushed.
They return alone to their residences.
No need to linger on the consequences,
too painful. Let's skip a month or so:
Gaia's off work. She decides to go
up and out to the roof of her building
to leaf through Lucian's *True History*,
listen to vaporwave on MP3,
and let the rays get started on gilding
(even though it's only May)
her limbs for their imminent summer display.

But really it's about the representation
of herself to herself. Of course, I don't know,
but I'd guess that in her imagination,
she's playing at being, like, Marilyn Monroe.
She has eyeliner on, her hair is done nicely,
and her nails and bikini match precisely,
though she must be expecting solitude,
since when she realizes there's a dude
standing on the roof of the building adjacent
lifting barbells of impressive size
(given his height) she gasps with surprise.
He hears her and turns, looking complacent.
Below his pectorals, matching scars
announce this Adonis is "one of ours."

He smiles at Gaia, all sweaty and brawny:
—"So, do you come up here a lot?"
As openings go it's kinda corny
but who cares about that when this guy's so hot?
—"Sometimes, you know, if I'm feeling reclusive."
—"Oh dude, I'm sorry, am I being intrusive?"
—"Not a bit! Don't worry, it's not a reproof,
you're fine! I mean, you're on your own roof!"
She laughs, betraying her agitation
but the guy seems willing to persevere.
He tries again: "It's nice up here."
—"It is! I like all the crenellation!"
—"The what?" —"The, like, castle-y bit."
—"Wow, yeah, I see it. Yeah, legit."

Gaia looks at her hand like she's going to bite it.
—"Sorry, ignore me, I'm being a freak."
—"You be you, you don't have to fight it.
Y'know, your perspective is just unique!
Individuality is something you have to treasure.
I'm Baker, by the way. It's a pleasure."
He smiles again, friendly and bright
showing his teeth, so neat and white.
—"I'm Gaia." —"Awesome! And you're my neighbor?
Rad. You're like, the trans femme next door!
So what do you do? Like, tell me more."
—"A sex toy store alienates my labor.
It's union though, so at least I'm insured.
And you?" —"I work at Callen-Lorde."

(On that: how come the non-profit sector
employs trans dudes so promiscuously?
I suppose they think if some sort of inspector
came round to assess their diversity
they're covered for transgender representation.
In trans academia the situation
is the same. All the men are tenure-track
but somehow us girls never hear back
from the search committee. I had the delusion
I could be a professor, so I got my degree:
I'm a shop assistant with a PhD!
Why aren't I included in all this inclusion?)
"But also," he continues, "I sometimes appear
in porn. But like, if it's feminist and queer."

Gaia gapes —"I think I've seen you!
Doing cowboy bondage in a Stetson hat,
and chaps and spurs? Could that have been you?"
—"Dude yeah, my specialty is scenes like that."
—"What was it called, maybe *Hogtie Ho-down?*"
—"Oh close! Yeah almost. *Guy Poon Showdown.*"
—"Oh yeah, that's it!" And so they converse
about their interest in matters perverse
for like twenty minutes, until Baker announces,
—"I have a date. I've gotta scram.
But you should follow me on Instagram.
I'm @urbancowboi." And off he bounces,
leaving Gaia unable to focus on her book.
If you ask me, she seems, as the kids say, "shook."

She decides to comply with his exhortation,
opens her Insta, checks out his pics.
His grid is the product of careful curation:
a shirtless selfie/landscape mix
that makes him appear both sexy and arty.
He's posted a flier for a queer dance party
called Daddy Issues. According to the text
it's an "Oedipal Experience." And it's happening next
Saturday! Gaia reposts it. "Who's going?"
She comments, and tags a variety
of "friends" including both Keiko and me.
I can't tell whether she does this knowing
that Keiko likes her. It ought to be clear.
Can she be that clueless? Has she no idea?

We can note her objectively hurtful action.
But Gaia's intentions remain obscure
and the impact came after a chain reaction:
nothing in morality is simple or pure.
When Keiko receives this communication
she stares at her phone, at the notification,
for literally minutes, then puts it away,
makes like she'll go about her day,
and then takes the damn thing back out of her pocket
(Can't someone call her? Can't her phone break?
Can't she somehow realize it's a mistake?)
and holds her thumb on the button to unlock it,
and follows the link to say she'll go,
then messages Gaia to let her know.

I wish I could stop her, but fate is fated.
She's already chosen. She's going to write.
She's falling in love, intoxicated
by visions of going out dancing all night
in basement rooms with sexy lighting
surrounded by queers. It must be exciting
to feel like you're part of the fashionable crowd
and I'd guess, for Keiko, that Gaia is endowed
with all of that glamour, that potential.
Or perhaps I'm projecting. Be that as it may
she sets out for the party on Saturday
early, and is caught in a sudden torrential
late spring downpour. She's soaked to the skin
by the time she finally makes it in.

Her makeup's smeared, her clothes are sopping,
she damply pays the entrance fee:
the room is not exactly hopping.
She glances around, then speedily
runs to the bathroom, and uses the dryer
on both her hair and her attire,
with mixed results. She fixes her face,
returns to the almost empty space,
and messages Gaia, who's like, —"Departing!
Be there in thirty! Wow, it's wet."
Thirty passes. She's not there yet,
but the perverts and geeks are finally starting
to arrive, in denim and gleaming Docs
and dog-tags, or collars with the cutest locks.

When Gaia finally makes an appearance
Keiko's been waiting an hour or more.
She wears Burberry platforms she got on clearance
and a tiny t-shirt with the slogan WHORE.
She's brought some friends, and gives a glancing
round of intros, then heads to the dancing.
Keiko follows, leans over, and shouts in her ear:
—"Is this a sex party?" —"Bless you, just queer!
I mean, I'm not saying nobody's screwing,
they probably have a blackout room,
or maybe they don't. But I'd assume."
—"What's that?" —"A darkened section for doing
you know, whatever." —"Oh got it. Alright.
So, um, like how did you find this night?"

—"Well!" Gaia halts, and starts enthusing,
"I was on my roof, and I met this dude."
—"This what?" —"This dude." —"Oh that was confusing!
I heard you say that you ate this food!
I was like, a picnic?" —"He was mesmerizing,"
Gaia interrupts, "and he was exercising,
shirtless" (they're surrounded by shirtless men)
"and well, he was flirty, he was definitely a ten,
so I stalked him a bit, and I think he's attending.
I'm sure he's gonna get here soon,
wait till you see him, you're going to swoon."
Keiko's expression is kind of heartrending
for just a second, then she smiles, —"Oh great."
She sticks close to Gaia. It starts to get late.

Still Baker's not there. Gaia checks his Insta.
There are photos of him having fun elsewhere.
—"Ugh, such a stupid desperate spinster!
Why did I come here?" She finds a chair
and plunks herself down, no longer so buoyant.
—"You couldn't know, you're not clairvoyant,
and anyway, it's been fun hanging out.
I enjoyed the dancing." Keiko still has to shout.
She looks exhausted. Gaia gives her a smile.
—"Oh Keiko, that's nice? You're very sweet."
She meets her eyes, and gets back to her feet:
"Wanna dance again? I could stay a while."
Keiko grins like a fire: —"Well, not for too long.
It's late. But I do really like this song."

And let's press pause, as they enter the dancing,
and leave them for a bit. It's for the best:
they both look happy. There's something entrancing
about a freeze-frame. It seems to suggest
that it's possible to preserve our jubilation
like candied flowers, through crystallization,
so that later when things inevitably go wrong
or the problems we secretly had all along
but ignored overwhelm us, that then the chatter,
the laughter, the moving closer while we dance,
the singular, overinterpreted glance
we thought about for days, will continue to matter.
But nothing matters. It comes on you fast,
drops through your fingers, and spring is past.

Posted 9th June by @Eunuch_Onegin in series The Call-Out
content warnings: nerds
tags: asexuals; vegans; lesbians; jism

al fresco enjoyments in clement weather
(5/14)

Rewind again. When the frosts finish
gibberellins encourage the seeds to grow
and as Kate's levels of estrogen diminish
she too feels stirrings down below.
Her testes go to work supplying
her body with T. It's mortifying:
what a germination to undergo!
And when the first shoots begin to show,
tentatively peeking above the soil,
on her face, on her chest, everywhere
out peek the stems of manly hair.
I'm assuming she's also in emotional turmoil.
Hormones fuck up your feelings too:
they change your body, but your body's you.

Aashvi has set out a plan, according
to which the next step is to joyfully confirm
an uptick in fertility. They've been recording
video of Kate's cum, looking for sperm
(there's a phone attachment, which holds the jism)
but in spite of Kate's monthly onanism
the sperm-test app (obscurely named YO)
keeps on asserting her levels are "low."
After five whole months of such insistence
Kate sits herself on the bathroom floor:
—"Maybe my junk doesn't work anymore.
I mean, my entire adult existence
I've been taking estrogen, like fifteen years.
So what if my sperm never reappears?"

—"But we knew this would happen. It's all as expected.
We discussed that this would be very slow.
You mustn't become so dejected.
This is a commitment . . ." —"I know, I know,
but Aashvi, it's weird, I feel so brittle,
like something's bending me, little by little
and I'm going to snap. I'm not serene.
It's like how I felt when I was seventeen.
I've even got zits. And it's hard to feel
hopeful. I'm sorry, I know, I'm upset,
but it's hard to believe we're going to get
to have a child. Like, that can't be real.
and if it's not then I don't know why
I can't shoot some hormones into my thigh."

—"I know that it's hard. But such a formulation
deresponsibilizes you. You forget you've grown
into an adult, you have skill, determination,
you are highly impressive, and you're not alone:
I'm here. I love you. Of course you're stressed,
but it is not the case that you've regressed
simply because of this chemical change.
Also perhaps we need to make strange
this idea about real. That if we're pursuing
this thought of making a new life live
we envisage it through homonormative
reproduction narratives. What we are doing
isn't 'having a child.' If such a frame
makes us unreal, let us change the name."

—"You can't just wave this away with theory."
—"I'm not! I'm only trying to suggest . . ."
—"But Aashvi, I'm out of juice. I'm weary.
I mean, I just feel like I need a rest."
Kate sighs. —"Oh such demonstrative sighing!
But I don't think I'm wrong. We should be trying
to remember that the body's possibility
is larger than discourse allows it to be.
So: I have tenure, my family are wealthy,
and even if I'm not what is seen as slim,
and refuse to go to the bloody gym,
I am still under forty, and extremely healthy . . ."
—"Yeah, so I guess you're good to go.
Just a pity I'm, like you say, slow."

—"Oh Kate, this isn't a fair accusation.
I wasn't attacking you." —"Yes. You're right.
I was overreacting, out of frustration.
So I'm sorry, okay? I'm being contrite.
But that's just it. I don't know whether
I can keep on holding my shit together
if this takes much longer." —"Oh love, come here."
Kate stands. They embrace. "Of course there's this fear."
—"So many fears. Like, there's your mother.
If you have a baby with me, she'll go nuts."
—"Please, no more with these ifs and buts.
We put one foot in front of the other.
I do not have time for all this despair."
—"Oh well, so now who's being unfair?"

And they might have been processing their emotions
in the bathroom forever (that's dykes for you)
amidst the shampoos and body lotions,
if Aashvi didn't have so much shit to do.
With predictably dramatic timing
her phone begins an insistent chiming
reminding her she should be elsewhere:
Aashvi's too important to care
about the second half of most conversations.
Off she goes. Kate looks pissed,
but she's just a freelance journalist
without any pressing assignations,
so she texts somebody. Who could it be?
That's right, gentle reader. She's texting me.

—"What's up?" she begins, "I'm agitated.
Wanna get a drink?" I see it, and reply:
—"I always want to be inebriated.
There's a Trans Ladies Picnic. I might stop by,
if you were there to give me a reason."
—"There's a picnic already?" —"First of the season.
It's in Prospect Park. It started at one."
—"Haven't been in ages. Sounds like fun."
—"You overstate. But there'll be drinking."
I'd been planning to try to write today
but I think, well, sometimes you just have to say
fuck it, I'm going to go and get stinking
drunk with some trannies in the open air,
so I commit: "I'll see you there."

But enough about me. This is Kate's drama.
She slips through the door, without goodbyes,
and presently the panorama
of the TLP assaults her eyes.
About twenty transsexuals are confusedly milling
around on the grass. There's a woman grilling
vegan hot dogs, two girls embrace
noisily on a blanket, someone brought a case
of Straw-Ber-Ritas and—so distressing—
people are drinking them. There's a girl on a lead,
a girl with cat ears, there's obviously weed,
there's a VR headset, there's a girl who's undressing
to show off her implants —"Look, they're new!"
Kate takes a moment. It's quite a view.

Then she ambles over, vaguely saluting
a few of the revelers along the way
and sits down by a group who are eagerly disputing
which Star Trek character is the biggest gay.
—"Remember when Jadzia had that flirtation
with her wife from her previous incarnation?"
—"Yeah that ruled, but it's still not as queer
as my OTP, which is Garak and Bashir!"
—"Well Picard's so ace, it's almost excessive."
—"He's heteroromantic. That means he's het."
—"Careful, the asexuals will be upset.
Calling people het is now oppressive."
—"Asexual discourse was a mistake.
Anyway, what about Rom and Jake?"

Kate doesn't attempt any intervention.
She makes a face, and then, with a sigh,
she turns away and shifts her attention
to another little group sitting nearby.
One girl is complaining about the vilification
she endured on her way to the subway station:
—"There's all these dudes who just stand about
outside the building, and they always shout
stuff at me. It's not even witty.
They're like 'looking fine!' And then they laugh.
It makes me feel like I'm going to barf.
I only just moved to this part of the city,
but I might have to leave. I don't even know.
Don't they have anywhere else to go?"

—"Men," her friend sympathizes,
"It's like they're territorial, like a spider or an owl,
and it's weird, but everyone normalizes
their behavior. I never realized how foul
men are, until after I, like, transitioned.
It really changes how you're positioned.
Things are so fucked up in this society
but when you're a girl you suddenly see
everything from like, an oppressed perspective."
Kate scowls again, and digs in her pack
and finds a beer, but turns out to lack
an opener, so she makes an ineffective
search for a tool that might do the trick:
all she turns up are a rock, and a stick.

She wanders over to the woman who's cooking
the processed alternative vegan meat
and stands there for several seconds looking
expectant. —"Do you want something to eat?"
the chef demands. Her facial expression
behind her sunglasses, suggests aggression.
—"I just need something to open my beer."
The woman pulls out her keyring. —"Here.
Don't think we've met. The name is Janet.
So you like the picnic? You having a blast?"
—"Oh, yeah. I've been to these in the past."
—"I was the one did the work to plan it,
so if you don't like it, I'm the one to tell."
—"Oh thanks! It seems like it's going well."

The woman's anger appears to lessen
slightly. —"None of these little punks
have thanked me for being their delicatessen.
Bunch of hungry ungrateful drunks.
But I guess someone's gotta do it.
Being trans sucks. If I've lived through it
it was only because of this sort of shit
and if you've had the benefit,
you owe something back." —"Agreed. For real.
I helped with Camp Trans, but years ago."
—"You helped with what?" —"The protest. You know."
—"It's new on me. So, you want a meal?"
Kate gives her a look of disbelief,
which changes, as she sees me arrive, to relief.

She runs to greet me. After hugs and effusions
("Oh man, it's been ages"; "Well you're looking great!")
I take her up on her earlier allusions:
—"It sounds like you've been in a bit of a state?"
—"A state? I guess, a state of depression.
Well okay, so listen, I have a confession:
I've gone off hormones. We're trying for a kid."
I keep my lack of surprise well hid:
—"OMG, that's great! Congratulations!"
—"I'm not sure I want one! I feel so alone,
and I fucking hate testosterone,
and now this picnic, like the conversations,
are making me think it's not just fear
of like, commitment. They need me here!"

—"I'm not sure I follow?" —"So this new generation
of trans girls, like all the ones at this
picnic today, need education
and I feel like I've just been really remiss:
their theory is unsophisticated,
they barely see gender and race as related,
they have an essentialist approach to identity . . .
There were older women who adopted me
when I was new, and there's a tradition
I'm part of, of radical feminist
transsexual dykes. It's why I exist,
It's all that got me through transition,
and it's something these girls also need.
Someone has to tell them what zines they should read!

Instead apparently I'm planning on spending
my energy on biological parenthood:
eighteen years carefully tending
to a cisgender kid, when my priority should
be my fucking sisters. What am I thinking?"
—"Fucking hell, Kate. We need to be drinking
for this conversation. You got more beer?"
She sounds insane, but she's being sincere,
I realize. She has this dedication
to virtue. It's a very lesbian trait,
and one I admire, but can't imitate.
I drink, and consider her declaration:
—"Okay, I get that you're under stress,
but trans community is always a mess."

—"I don't believe in your pessimism.
I think you just pose as a misanthrope."
—"Let's say I'm suspicious of separatism.
You might be putting too much hope
in this vision of us looking after each other,
or of being some fuck-up's tranny mother.
I mean, we're okay, but that can't be all,
this community is simply way too small."
—"What's the alternative? Assimilation?
Inclusion is just a transparent device
to get us, in return for the promise of a slice
of privilege, to consent to our co-optation,
and to help to govern our own form of life."
—"Yeah, says the one with the rich cis wife."

—"She's not my wife! We aren't married."
I try for some levity. —"Oh bitch, like, please,
there's no need for you to sound so harried.
I get it. Okay. Your girlfriend. Your squeeze."
—"No, I mean, I'm not downplaying
how important she is, I'm only saying,
well, Aashvi's amazing, she's funny, and kind,
and hella clever, like, a brilliant mind,
and we love each other, but there's limitations.
There's stuff that you and I know and share
that she just doesn't. That sounds unfair.
I'm being a bitch." —"Self-flagellations
are unnecessary. You're safe. I'm your friend.
So, is your relationship about to end?"

—"Is that how it sounds?" —"Well you sort of implied . . ."
—"I mean, I hope not. Oh, I don't know.
It's true I'm feeling dissatisfied,
but I do love Aashvi. I love her so."
—"I'm only asking for clarification.
Do you want encouragement or commiseration?
I mean, I get that you're freaking out
but if you're not, actually, about
to upend your life, my recommendation
is to quit this picnic, and go to a bar.
I know a good one, not too far.
You need some rest and relaxation.
A girls' night out. What do you say?"
Kate smiles. —"Yeah. You're right. Okay."

As we leave, the sun kisses our arses.
The picnic's ending, it's the end of spring,
over, like everything that passes,
which is to say, like everything.
Spring begins, and things start growing,
you blink, it's May, and spring is going,
summer's upon you, it gets too hot,
ripeness is just the beginning of rot,
but not quite yet. First there's talking
and laughing in the bar, watching the light
in the windows fading. Then there's the night.
We devour some pizza, and then start walking,
and reluctantly take our separate ways
to sleep, to wake to summer days.

Posted 7th July by @Eunuch_Onegin in series The Call-Out
content warnings: Philadelphia
tags: trucks; Genesis; capitalism

an annual community get-together
(6/14)

And summer appears as a profusion:
rhododendrons, roses, peonies, all
bloom in defiance of the inevitable conclusion
that their thick petals will wither and fall.
Summer's too much, it's always tipping
over. The bushes keep needing clipping,
the weeds keep needing to be pulled from the ground,
the ants and flies unstoppably abound,
feeding, then breeding. Summer is excessive,
it repeats, it diverts, it finds a way
and it doesn't listen to a thing you say.
Day has also been acting transgressive.
Somewhere within her she's been getting strong,
and strength can never be contained for long.

She returns, one Thursday night in early
August, from work in a difficult mood.
Her manner could politely be described as surly:
almost as if she's trying to be rude.
She comes in the door and, without saying
anything, sits down and commences playing
the switch, as if totally unaware
that Bette is home, and sitting right there.
Bette considers a moment, then offers a greeting:
—"Hi." But still Day doesn't reply.
Bette tries again. "Day! I said hi."
—"Okay, I heard you, I'm busy beating
this lynel. Just chill. I won't be long."
—"You're acting weird. Is something wrong?"

—"Okay, alright, I'll let it kill me.
You happy now?" —"What's going on?"
—"I'm trying to relax. Do you have to grill me?
I get enough questions all day when I'm gone."
She breathes. "I told my boss I'm quitting."
—"No you didn't! You're fucking shitting."
—"I did. He, like, misgendered me twice,
I know I'm supposed to ignore it and be nice,
but I told him it was discrimination
and that I was leaving, and that he was a jerk.
I'm sorry. I can maybe find freelance work,
I mean, I still have a qualification."
—"Oh fuck. Please tell me this isn't true."
—"You know what? I'm glad. It's the right thing to do!"

—"But Day . . ." —"It's like I'm trapped. I'm living
the same stupid life I lived as a boy!
It sucks. I've had enough of giving
up pleasure for money. I deserve more joy!"
—"Day, calm down, you're being silly."
—"Bette, will you come with me to Philly?
This weekend's the weekend of PTHC
and I found an apartment on Airbnb . . ."
—"You quit your job, you fail to tell me,
which okay, whatever, it's a mistake
but I guess it's one you get to make,
but then you decide to try and sell me
on a fucking vacation." She can only groan.
—"Well fine. I'm going on my own!"

(Does PTHC need explanation?
Are any cisgenders reading this thing?
It's a conference some medical organization
puts on every year in order to bring
together professionals working in the field
of making transsexuals pay to be "healed":
surgeons, psychiatrists, frauds of that sort.
But it turned out the conference also brought
their "clients" to town, in unexpected
numbers. Some of us paid the fee
and participated, but increasingly we
have skipped the formalities and instead elected
to simply treat it as a chance
to gather, and drink, and fuck, and dance.)

Relatedly, elsewhere, Gaia is walking
to work. While weaving sure and quick
through the crowd, she's simultaneously stalking
Baker online. He's posted a pic
of himself and his truck. Below he enquires
as to whether anyone he knows desires
a ride to Philly. She stops mid stride
(behind her several people collide)
as if struck by lightning. And then there's a second
stroke, a message: —"Hey, do you know
about this conference in Philly? I think I might go,
Have you been? Is it good? I sort of reckoned
we could go together, maybe, if you're free."
Oh Keiko, you're acting so predictably!

But whatever, to Gaia it must seem exciting
to be pursuing and also pursued.
So she sets it up, but somehow, in writing
to Keiko she carelessly forgets to include
a crucial detail—the name of who's driving—
and it's still unclear upon Baker's arriving
at Keiko's apartment. When the truth comes out,
Keiko's clearly upset, but she doesn't pout.
Instead she calls shotgun, almost literally throwing
her body between her crush and the guy
her crush is crushing. But then Baker says —"Hi,"
all friendly, and asks, "Your first time going?"
and she has to reply. —"Um, yeah." —"Oh neat!
It's, like, transformative. You're in for a treat."

—"I'm not sure I need a transformation."
—"Yeah, dope, you seem like an awesome chick,
but it's like, a powerful recalibration
to be in a space where you just, like, click,
you know what I'm saying?" —"Um, not really."
—"Well like, where everyone, or nearly,
is the same as you. You look around,
and you're not looking, you're just, like, found."
—"The same as me? Will everyone be arty?
Or Asian?" —"Well sure, but you know what I mean.
Trust me, you'll feel really seen.
Plus, it's also just a radical party."
He's looking increasingly bewildered and hurt,
but Keiko's not folding: —"I'm an introvert."

The situation's in need of decompression,
and even Gaia gets the gist.
She decides to attempt an intercession:
—"It's still important for this conference to exist,
I mean, whatever our variation.
If I want to discuss Latin translation,
there are conferences for that, so there ought to be
one centered on transsexuality.
And I'm excited. It's my first visit.
Hey Baker, how many times have you been?
—"Been every year since twenty-thirteen."
—"Oh wow, amazing. So tell us, how is it?"
—"Oh right, it's awesome. Last year I went
to like five of the panels." —"Did you present?"

—"I did! I gave a presentation
on a panel called 'Unbearable Privilege'
about how we have female socialization,
but also we're dudes, and so how do you bridge
your experience of oppression before you were male,
with the way as a man you now totally sail
past all those problems. That hurts as well,
you know, 'cause of guilt. Guilt is like, hell.
Oh man, like, gender is complicated."
I'm sure Gaia has an analysis
to hand to critique a take such as this,
but then things might have re-escalated,
so for once, she's tactful. For the rest of the drive.
Keiko stares out the window. At last, they arrive.

Kate and myself also decided
to attend the conference. It was her idea.
We travel by bus—I know, misguided—
then walk to the venue. I can tell we're near
when I realize I've started recognizing
about half the pedestrians, but it's still surprising
to walk into the conference hall,
which is full of people, and see that all
of them are trans. I was so isolated,
back in the nineties, I was told my life
would be lived "on the sharp edge of a knife"
and believed it. How unsophisticated!
A naïve child, who couldn't foresee
that "trans" would become a commodity.

I'm in a huge hall filled with tables
each acting as a sort of impromptu shop
covered in gaudy banners and labels.
They rent for five hundred dollars a pop.
Teenagers known for their tireless vlogging
take selfies with fans, while their assistants are flogging
them t-shirts to help them be "proud but stealth."
Other uses for our limited reserves of wealth
include dildos, books, jewelry, stickers,
herbal supplements, voice-training kits,
binders, packers, silicone tits,
therapy, chocolates, boxers and knickers
with the trans symbol, in case you forget . . .
and like every year, it's the biggest yet.

Our other acquaintances are variously dotted
throughout this queerly commercial scene.
Baker, on entry, is immediately spotted
by like eight people who'd totally been
hoping he'd be here, so after extending
a reminder to Gaia that she should be attending
a party that night called "Bits 'n' Tits"
and telling her that she's a babe, he splits.
Gaia beams. —"So girl, have you ever
seen such a babe?" —"I guess it was kind
That he drove, but he's like, not very . . . clever?
Or maybe I'm wrong!" —"Oh fuck his mind!
I don't go to men for their intellects,
but well, I mean, have you seen his pecs?"

She laughs, and they browse for a bit, before sighting
Kate and myself. Gaia makes straight
for us with a greeting. —"This is so exciting!
You're here as well!" She turns to Kate.
"Hi, I'm Gaia. I follow you on Twitter,
your writing's brilliant." Kate gives a titter,
and averts her eyes: —"Oh, flattery."
—"It's not! Your work is important to me!
It's satirical trans interpretation
of culture. I love your analysis
of how Peter Gabriel from Genesis
was secretly representing trans alienation
in the midst of all that prog excess
by wearing a fox mask and his wife's red dress."

—"Oh yeah, Phil Collins fucking hated
the fact he did that. And he wanted to wear
it all the time. It's like he created
this monstrous feminine nightmare
out of papier-mâché and women's clothing
to stage his own submerged self-loathing
and it was still much better than being a man.
You just have to be the woman you can."
—"And being that woman has to mean embracing
our monstrous nature. Like, you have to be
yourself. That's just a tautology.
There's this trope of destroying yourself and replacing
yourself with another . . ." —"Which of course isn't true!"
—"And that's totally something I learned from you!"

While this extempore love-in is ensuing
I'm left with Keiko. We've met before,
like twice. I venture —"So how're you doing?"
What the fuck's her name? I'm just not sure.
What is she? A student? But then, my salvation
from this awkward beginning to a conversation
comes in the unlikely form of Day,
who bounces up. —"Oh hi there, hey!"
She asks Keiko her name, proceeds to look up
her profile on Twitter and elsewhere online,
tries to guess her astrological sign,
then asks, "So are you here to hook up?
I am. The flirting here is extreme.
So many cuties. It's like a dream."

—"I'm not sure I'm very good at flirtation.
I'm like, the unrequited passion sort."
—"Well, what you need is an education.
Flirting's a skill, and it can be taught.
I used to be shy, but then I got better.
Now I'm a real sexual go-getter!"
—"Oh well, I mean, I suppose you could try.
But like, I mean, it's not that I'm shy,
it's more a problem of communication,
like nobody receives the signals I put out.
Am I being too subtle? But I don't want to shout."
—"Believe me, I totally understand that frustration.
I was always quiet. And yeah, it's strange
at first to be louder, but it's possible to change."

Keiko is wearing a skeptical expression
but Day's undeterred. "The important thing
is you don't give up. You can't let depression
or doubt or fear or whatever bring
you down. At first it's terrifying,
like who would fuck me? But you keep on trying,
and you realize you're someone people want to fuck."
—"Well, my personality must suck
or I must be ugly. I never make it."
—"Don't you think other trannies are hot?"
—"Well, yeah. But I guess I'm the one who's not."
—"You're very cute! I'm sorry to break it
to you, but you're not a special case."
—"Then what's the problem? Is the problem race?"

Day startles, and even pauses for a second.
—"You mean, that you're Asian?" —"Could that be true?"
—"Oh right. I see. But I wouldn't have reckoned . . .
I mean every tranny is a weeaboo,
no shade, me too, and like, racism's real,
but I think that plenty of them would feel
like, into the fact you're . . . Japanese?"
Day smiles. She looks so eager to please.
Keiko stares at her. For a moment they're quiet.
Then Day moves on. "Well, you should go
to the reading tonight. It's that press, you know,
that publishes trannies? It'll be a riot,
There are awesome readers, and it'll be packed.
It's a perfect chance to . . . interact."

Gaia turns —"I heard about that reading,
I'll definitely come." Then Kate: —"Me as well!"
I consider taking her aside and pleading
that literary events are literally hell:
the discomfort, the forced applause, the pretension,
the novelists possessed of the misapprehension
that we'd like them to read their entire book
slowly, in a monotone, without a look
up at the audience, the poets reciting
formless nonsense in a sonorous voice . . .
they indulge themselves, and you have no choice,
you just have to sit and listen to their "writing,"
no intermission and no reprieve:
abandon hope, it's impossible to leave!

Then I think, Day's right. The reason for going
isn't the reading, but the company,
and there's nothing much to be gained from showing
my grouchiness to Kate, so I decide to be
delighted at the plan. —"That sounds amusing."
Kate smiles. She's glad I'm not refusing,
and I'm glad to please her. The last month or two
we've hung out a lot. What can you do?
An old friend calls, her relationship's ropy,
you spend time, it's pleasant, you remember you care
about their happiness, then worse, about their
opinion of you. Well, call me dopey,
but as Kate and I exit the air-con for the street
even sweaty summer seems kind of sweet.

Posted 16th August by @Eunuch_Onegin in series The Call-Out
content warnings: publishers; folding chairs
tags: manga; silence; literature; cats

transsexual literature takes the stage
(7/14)

A summer evening in the unwinding city.
It's not yet dark, although the sun
is behind the buildings. Everything shitty
looks better in the dusk. The work-week's done,
people are leaving their offices, milling
around the parks and pavements, and filling
the drinking establishment patios,
but their voices are gentle. It's like everything slows
down on these evenings, like the air is thicker,
or the light is heavy. The barest breeze
crawls through the squares, where below the trees
the incautious fireflies hover and flicker,
gathering, as the people are gathering too,
just as incautious, with the same end in view.

Amidst all this various recreation
Kate and I are wending our way
to the anarchist bookstore that provides the location
for the trans lit reading. —"So Kate," I say,
"What do you make of that girl, Gaia?"
—"She seems fine, I guess." —"Oh whatever, you liar!
You loved it when she fangirled at you."
—"I'm happy my stuff is getting through,
although it's weird she called it satire.
I guess I make jokes. But I'm trying to not.
They're just too safe." —"You're trying to what?"
—"To be more serious. Or like, my desire
is to do some writing where I don't revoke
my meaning by making it into a joke."

—"But like, if a piece of writing is comical
you both mean it and don't. So the statement can be
like, denser, more complex, and more economical."
—"I guess I've lost faith in 'complexity.'
Oppression is simple." So the conversation
continues till we reach our destination.
Meanwhile, as they move down a parallel street
Gaia is seizing the chance to entreat
Keiko to give her more information
about her work —"So like how did you start
learning to do this kind of art?
Like why is it prints? And representation?"
—"Well I like to draw." —"Oh obviously. Sure.
but why in this style? There must be more."

—"Well as far as why it's realistic,
I don't get why you wouldn't be.
My parents are lawyers, they're not artistic,
but how things look is just interesting to me,
When I was a kid I was always drawing . . .
but I should shut up, I'm being boring."
—"Are you kidding? You're a genius, you dork.
I promise, I want to hear you talk.
Like, tell me stuff. Please keep on going."
—"Well so I'm interested in how stuff looks,
and I was really into comic books,
like, exaggeration as a means of showing
like the shapes or essences that underlie
the complexity of things, like a thing's *jittai* . . ."

—"*Quidditas* I think is the Latin phrasing."
—"Um, yeah. Well anyway, when I was eight
I was reading Hergé, which I thought was amazing,
and like, sure he's racist, but his art is so great,
and also Jeff Smith, and then someone bought me,
my uncle I think, some manga, which taught me
a lot. It was different, it wasn't from the West,
it wasn't American. I became obsessed
with trying to draw like Taiyo Matsumoto,
Then I started to ask, where did he learn?
Did the person I'm copying copy in their turn?
One thing about drawing, why it's different from a photo,
is that style has a history, so when you draw
you're in touch with everyone who's drawn before."

—"But there's a history of choices about style
that's also going on in photography."
—"That's true. But drawing's more versatile,
you don't just click to turn what you see
into an image. So in terms of expressing . . .
okay, I'm a Luddite, fine, I'm confessing.
I hate photography and it isn't fair."
—"Oh hey, there's the bookshop, we're almost there."
—"That's kind of a pity. I liked us walking."
—"I'm sorry, my fault! I walk too fast!
And like, you're not wrong. About art and the past."
—"Oh yeah. It's weird for me, to be talking
about these opinions I usually hide . . ."
and chatting away, they go inside.

I'm already in there, unhappily seated
on a folding chair. They're starting late.
People are standing, we're all overheated
and sticky and smelly, and we have to wait.
The woman who seems to be organizing
keeps turning to the crowd and apologizing
—"Sorry, we'll start as soon as we can!"
I know her a little, but I'm not a fan;
she's always so bouncy and energetic.
Gets on my tits. She's English too,
and she thinks she's charming, but I see through
her act: the friendly and hyperkinetic
ingénue, who's doing her best.
It's exhausting. Like, lady, give it a rest.

Another twenty minutes passes:
at last the guy who owns the press
appears, in chinos and mirrored glasses,
to the evident relief of our perky hostess.
She hums in the microphone, bites her nails,
says "excuse me" a lot, and finally prevails
on the room to be quiet. —"Wow, what a crowd!
This is so exciting! Hurrah! I'm so proud!
This is such an amazing celebration
of our writing, of us, of who we are.
And now I give you, Rod François,
our publisher, and our inspiration!
Everyone, clap! Give Rod a big hand!"
and she skips away from the microphone stand.

Then Rod comes up, his glasses glistening.
He doesn't remove them. He starts to sway.
Is he high? —"Hello. Are you all listening?
I'm glad so many of you are here today,
Because as of now, you're part of a movement
that uses writing as a tool for the improvement
of the world! I know that of course it looks
like what we do is make great trans books,
and we do! You've all read *Arizona*?
And what did you think? Was it fucking great?
Were you like, 'It's a book, but I somehow relate'?
Turns out a novel about a tranny stoner
driving to Flagstaff can also be
a tool to build community!

"People think that the power of books is surprising,
like 'it's just a book.' Well I've got news!
Books are vital. We need humanizing
depictions of ourselves, depictions we can use,
to feel okay, or make sense of our being.
Because if you're cis, you're used to seeing
people like you in books and on screen.
That's normal, that's how it's always been.
But we have to do the work of trying
to insert ourselves, and pretend we can see
meaning in characters we could never be,
and failing, and feeling like we're lying,
or else we conclude that books are lame
and go off to play a computer game.

"And simultaneously, we're learning
we have nothing to say, that people of our kind,
whatever emotions we might have churning
around in our bodies, don't have a mind:
we can't be authors, we needn't be respected,
at best we're specimens to be dissected!
Know yourself, the philosophers instruct,
unless you're trans, in which case, you're fucked.
We're known by others. Our prescribed aspiration
is to change ourselves, the definition of despair!
Worse yet, we don't know what it is we share.
Because of our intellectual isolation
we're strangers to each other, a community without
any real culture to talk about."

He pauses, in a way that might be dramatic
or might be him just losing his thread,
strokes his glasses, then with an emphatic
gesture removes them. His eyes are red,
and sort of puffy. His pupils are tiny.
"I don't like to sit around being a whiny
little bitch. So if something is shit
my question is what do we do about it?"
He replaces his glasses. "Our ambition,
me and my ex, when we started this thing,
was that books could be a way to bring
people together, build a coalition,
which then we could use to make real change . . .
doing this without her is really strange."

He pauses again. "We had some friction.
But we always worked through it. We built trans lit.
Basically we invented transgender fiction!
And if you're successful then people will shit
on you. But you know, they couldn't ignore us.
We changed the game. What was here before us?
The problems began when things got good.
She wanted to fail. She thought she should . . .
I believed I could fix all these broken crazy
brilliant women, if I could get this press,
this book, this movement, to be a success.
Give them reasons to live. But people are lazy.
They don't like it if you try to make them do
things for themselves. They turn on you."

Our hostess is looking increasingly worried.
She shifts in her seat, and gestures snip-snip,
but the man doesn't notice, or won't be hurried:
he starts to discuss his relationship
with feminism, and with his mother
and has dropped that story, and is starting another
when she interrupts. Then one by one
she brings up the authors, who all overrun
their allotted times. It's like they're competing
to be the most boring. One reads in a drone,
one can't seem to find her story on her phone,
one tells us she's discovered, after completing
an online test, she's part Cherokee,
then reads a piece about astrology.

Then there's a lady who insists on silence
for three whole minutes, to commemorate
"our murdered sisters." The only violence
I find myself able to contemplate
is against her person. At last they're finished.
our hostess, her energy undiminished,
makes us all clap. She's a maniac.
Gaia and Keiko are standing at the back
so they get out quickly. Gaia is barely
containing her excitement. —"Come on, let's move!
Bits 'n' Tits! Let's get in the groove.
It's an all-trans night! That happens so rarely,
but when it does, it's always so fun!"
She swings from a sign, and takes off at a run.

Keiko hesitates, but just for a flicker,
then she laughs, and starts to run as well.
Gaia has a lead, but Keiko's quicker:
the two of them speed down the street pell-mell,
Keiko overtakes, Gaia grabs her fingers,
she spins around, the moment lingers,
then Gaia laughs, and Keiko does too.
—"Oh Keiko," Gaia says, "I have fun with you.
You're fun and interesting and clever.
I'm glad you came. We talk about stuff.
Like real ideas. I don't do that enough."
—"I'm glad as well! I'd normally never
attend an event with 'health' in the name."
—"Oh my god, yeah. Health is so lame!"

—"It is!" —"But it's really for socializing."
—"Right! And socializing's healthy for me.
Which, given the fact I'm criticizing
this conference for its health, is an irony.
But it's joy, not health, that I desire:
and I like you too. I like you, Gaia."
She blushes. And then they're at the queue
and someone's shouting —"Hey! You two!"
It's Baker. He's drunk. His enunciation
is careful and heavy. "I've got VIP.
I'll get you in." They're about to agree,
when a very unfortunate realization
dawns on Keiko —"I forgot my ID!
I'll have to go get it from the Airbnb!"

Back at the reading, I'm stuck and surrounded
by a surging crowd in the tiny room.
All the readers are being hounded
by fans, who seem to want to consume
them whole, as if their temporary glamour
could be gnawed and digested. My god, the clamor!
I'm so desperate to leave I even ignore
the table of wine, as I push to the door,
though I notice that Day is standing by it
quaffing some rosé, and talking at
a lady who read about her cat.
I hear Day tell her —"You should try it!"
That's Day. I think. She'll always try
too hard, and it makes things go awry.

At least this writer, who's slightly older
than most of the others, pale and tall,
with straight blond hair that falls to her shoulder
(the only half-decent reader of all)
is being indulgent, or perhaps forbearing,
listening to whatever Day is sharing,
(boast, contention, confession of sin,
appeal for approval?) with a cryptic grin.
Outside, Kate grabs me, and starts advancing
away down the street. "Let's go back to that park,"
she suggests, "we can sit on a bench in the dark.
Decompress for a bit, before we go dancing."
—"You mean the square?" —"The square, yeah, right.
It looked like a nice place to be at night."

And it is. We do a little exploring
and inspect the fireflies, the trees, the moon,
then sit. I say —"That event was boring,
and Rod François is such a buffoon.
So much vaunting, so little attainment.
So shoddy! They call that entertainment?
We get it, you're representing our womanhood
but your work still has to actually be good."
Kate laughs. —"Oh please, relax with the judging.
They're young. I'm sure they're working on it.
And *Arizona*'s good, you have to admit."
—"It's okay," I say. I'm being begrudging.
Actually I loved it. —"You loved it," Kate says.
"You wouldn't shut up about it for days."

She knows me so well. And she's not mistaken.
I am ridiculous. She looks in my eyes,
and I look in hers, and I feel quite shaken.
It's like all of a sudden we recognize
each other, at last. What are we doing?
We're friends, we're mates, we shouldn't be screwing
that up! And then I say —"Um, Kate,"
and she says, —"Yes," and the rest is fate,
or choice, or whatever. First there's the leaning,
the touching of hands, the —"Hang on, this . . .",
the —"I know, it isn't . . .", and then the kiss.
It's just a moment, it has no meaning,
no-one knows, and it's over so soon,
Surrounded by fireflies, lit by the moon.

Posted 12th September by @Eunuch_Onegin in series The Call-Out
content warnings: consent issues; repetitive music; flashing lights
tags: sweat; stairs; whisky; hats

a disco full of lust and rage
(8/14)

But now let's leave that joy or sorrow
behind in the darkness. The least that's said,
the soonest mended. Come back tomorrow.
What's done is done. We'll turn instead
to Keiko, who's passionately sprinting
back to the club, the sweat glinting
on her brow and limbs, and soaking her shirt.
She's really panting. Her lungs must hurt.
And then, at last, after breathlessly getting
to the club, the bouncer won't let her go straight
to the front of the line. She has to wait.
She's not on the list. It must be upsetting,
I'd guess, for a person who runs so fast
to be halted. But whatever, she gets in at last.

The venue is one of those complicated
types, with doors, and stairs, and nooks,
and various dancefloors, all populated
with gyrating transsexuals. Keiko looks
in all of them. People keep on greeting
her warmly. She doesn't remember meeting
any of them before. Perhaps they're just high.
She smiles politely and squeezes by
through the dry ice, the strobe lighting,
and the autotune vocals by Britney Spears,
over floors sticky with spilt beers,
and goes around twice before finally sighting
Gaia, who's lurking in the topmost space
in a corner, sucking on Baker's face.

Keiko stares, then turns, like she's fleeing,
then turns again, like she's going to stay.
As she turns again she sees Gaia seeing
her turning around. Gaia breaks away
from the kiss with Baker. For a couple of seconds
she hesitates too, but then she beckons
Keiko over, and shouts in her ear
—"That took so long! But I'm glad you're here!
Look at this party! The place is jumping!
Do you want a drink?" —"No, thanks, I'm fine."
Then Baker asks —"Were you stuck in the line?
I'm sorry!" He's slurring his words and slumping.
It's clear he's been partying hard all night.
Keiko turns to Gaia —"Is he alright?"

—"He's fine." —"He seems like he's having trouble."
—"Well yeah, but it's Philly. It's like, you're meant
To be wasted. We're all in this bubble!"
—"But then, if he's drunk, how can he consent?"
Gaia just laughs, like the thought is amusing.
—"Don't laugh! Don't you remember refusing
to kiss me that time we went on that date
because you said it would violate
my consent because of the fact I'd been drinking?"
—"I don't . . . I think you misconstrued . . .
That wasn't a date, and Baker's a dude,
it's a different dynamic . . . oh fuck, you're still thinking
about that night. I didn't intend
to make you unhappy. I mean, you're my friend."

—"Well it didn't seem like you were looking
for friendship, back when we kissed at New Year."
—"Oh Keiko, listen I enjoyed us hooking
up, or whatever. But like, we're queer.
We hook up with friends, that's just normal:
like, things don't have to be so formal . . ."
—"Okay but you lied to me about why
you wouldn't kiss me. I felt like I
was out of control, or maybe crazy . . ."
—"Okay, I might have made a mistake,
But I'm not a liar, I'm not, like, fake . . .
My memories of New Year are honestly hazy
but I really like you, I honesty do,
we're friends, and that's not fake, it's true."

Gaia takes a step forward. It looks like she's trying
to offer a hug, in the most awkward way.
Keiko looks like she might start crying.
Neither seems to know what to say.
Gaia glances back. "Oh god, I hate this.
Come on, don't exaggerate this.
Let me get you a drink? Like, let's not fight.
This event is so good. Let's enjoy the night."
—"I think I should go. I should be leaving."
—"No you should stay . . ." —"It's for the best.
I think I'm tired. I need some rest."
And like that she's gone, speedily weaving
between the dancers. Over and out.
Baker leans in. —"What was that about?"

Keiko moves deftly, but the crowd's an obstruction.
She squeezes past a woman who's dressed
like an extra from an amateur production
of *Phantom of the Opera*, then one in distressed
futuristic armor of her own fabrication,
then one in a matching combination
of tie-dyed leotard, mask and gloves,
all dancing like crazy. She pushes and shoves,
and the exit sign has entered her vision,
when she hears a voice —"Hey Keiko, hey!"
She turns around, and sees that it's Day,
and has just a second to make a decision.
She lets her eyes meet the other's eyes.
Day smiles, "Oh hi." —"Oh hi," she replies.

Is her "hi" too perky, is she smiling too brightly?
Who knows what it is that gives her away,
but Day seems to pause, and then frowns slightly,
then asks —"Hey Keiko, are you okay?
You seem kinda sad?" —"Oh please, don't worry!"
—"You seemed to be . . . in kind of a hurry?"
—"I'd just decided it was time to go."
—"Already?" Keiko sighs. —"Well, so,
I've been, like, tragically infatuated
with this girl. With Gaia. But she seems to be . . .
we're friends, but she's totally oblivious to me,
which is why I've been feeling so frustrated
about, like, flirting." Another sigh.
"And now she's upstairs kissing some guy."

—"Well clearly she doesn't know what she's missing.
Not to be rude, but you're sexy as fuck,
and if she's with some dude when she could be kissing
a girl, she's either shit out of luck,
or straight, which is worse." Keiko smiles and blushes,
so Day plunges on: "I mean I've had crushes
on people who didn't like me back
and I used to think it was because of some lack
in me, like I was bad and defective,
and they turned me down because they could see
whatever it was that was wrong with me,
like their judgement was somehow objective . . .
but who cares if Gaia likes you or not?
You just need someone to think you're hot."

—"Well, sure, okay, but that's not the only
reason I like her. It's not just about me,
and actually I'm fine with being lonely,
that's all I was until recently.
But Gaia's an intellectual. She's clever,
we can talk about things, and like, I've never
had friends like that so much. She knows
all this cool stuff, like clubs and shows.
or even stupid things, we were playing
this game called Whisky Slaps, where you . . ."
—"Oh Whisky Slaps! I love that too!
Shall we do a round? Don't worry, I'm paying."
Keiko blushes, looks at the floor,
then looks back up and says, —"Yeah, sure."

Day buys two Maker's. —"This stuff's delicious!"
They're doubles. Keiko does a shot,
then bam! Day slaps her. She's pretty vicious.
—"Oh wow," Day says, "that was kind of hot."
She laughs self-consciously. Keiko starts shaking
her head in circles. —"Oof! It's aching.
You really hit me!" She smiles at Day.
"Alright, it's your turn. Ready to play?"
Day drinks and tenses in anticipation.
Keiko slaps her. —"You hit like a chick!
Come on, slap like you've got a dick."
—"I don't think my junk has any relation
to how hard I hit." —"So give me a slap!
Like, use your wrist. It's all in the snap."

Keiko slaps her again, still quite lightly,
Day laughs. "I think I felt that sting!
Owee! No, for real, that was slightly
better, but I get it, this isn't your thing."
She grins. "You prefer receiving a bruising . . ."
Keiko blushes again. —"Well, it's confusing
I don't know, it's so hard to get clear in your head
About what you want, you know, in bed . . .
I used to think I was ace or aro
because I found it hard to identify
with any kind of sex where I was a guy,
but even as a girl, the range is so narrow . . ."
—"Ask me, it sounds like you overthink.
What you need is action. Another drink?"

And then she turns, without even waiting
for Keiko to answer, and orders more booze.
"You can't just hang round vacillating
forever. Like, what have you got to lose?
I mean we're just trannies. People hate us.
The cis would like to eliminate us
and every day that we survive
it's like, a bonus. To being alive!"
She gulps her drink in a single swallow.
Keiko does too. —"Oh wow, that's strong."
A song comes on —"I love this song!"
Day says —"Let's dance! I'll lead, you follow."
She takes Keiko's hand, does a pirouette,
then pulls her off through the bodies and sweat.

Once in the crowd attempts at style,
or even a simple *pas-de-deux*
can only last a little while,
and if you're dancing in a two
you end up in a juxtaposition
inherently suggestive of possible coition.
That's the whole point. That's why you're there.
Day gently brushes Keiko's hair
and looks in her eyes, with a beckoning smile.
Keiko gives a gasp. —"Oh, I see."
—"What?" says Day, "you're attractive to me.
You seem so pure. I'd like to defile
your innocence, at least a bit.
At least, that is, if you're into it?"

Keiko blinks, —"I guess, yeah, maybe . . ."
Day moves her head forward and touches her lips
to Keiko's lips. —"Well shush then, baby,"
she murmurs gently, and then she slips
her tongue in her mouth and her fingers into
the pockets of her jeans, so she can begin to
tug their hips together, close . . .
I should tell you that I feel extremely gross
recounting all this in such detail,
but it's clear that how you act during sex
has moral value, and that it reflects
on your general character. I must not fail
to record information that, sadly, is key
to the drift of this story, out of modesty.

So please don't take me as being lubricious
when I say that Day is overcome by lust
or rather (to not be injudicious)
that she acts like she is, since we can't trust
our eyes, I mean, she could be pretending.
In any case, after spending
a number of minutes—twenty? ten?—
kissing, then grinding, then kissing again,
then squeezing and pinching, then humping and bucking,
she comes up for air. —"Oh, you turn me on.
You wanna fuck? We could go to the john?
Or maybe right here! I feel like fucking
in public's exciting. Is it? Or no?
Maybe the bathroom? Like, take it slow?"

—"Um, we could go to where I'm staying.
Gaia won't be there. It's pretty near . . ."
—"And leave this party? This is what I've been praying
to have my whole life, and now I'm here
and I want it all. I want to be doing
whatever there is. Including screwing.
And it's single stall. Don't be scared."
—"I'm not, I'm just, like . . . unprepared?"
—"Well then, get ready!" Day's highly excited,
giggling and bouncing, and it seems Keiko gets
into the spirit. She laughs as she lets
Day push her into the poorly lighted
bathroom, covered in felt-pen scrawl,
and slam her up against the wall.

—"Wait, hey wait, the door needs locking."
—"Oh shit, it does." Day flicks it shut
and then commences vigorously defrocking
both Keiko and herself. She grabs Keiko's butt
and pulls down her jeans, all while biting
her on the neck, and also fighting
to remove the tights she unadvisedly chose
to wear tonight. Her pantyhose
at length half-masted, and the liberation
of her turgid, Cialis-fueled clit
finally achieved, she spreads some spit
on Keiko's anus, for lubrication.
—"Wait," slurs Keiko, "is that, like, spit?"
—"Yeah, for your butt, when I'm destroying it."

—"Wait, hold on, I'm not sure it . . .
I mean . . . I've never had butt sex before . . ."
—"It's good for you. You'll adore it.
I'll fuck you like a little whore."
—"But will it hurt?" Day grins. —"Kinda.
But pain you'll like." —"Well I don't mind a
bit of pain. Okay, let's try."
Day puts it in. Keiko gives a cry.
—"Ow! Ow stop! It's excruciating!"
Day stops. —"I've stopped, are you okay?
I was only it in a little way."
—"Ow, fuck. It felt so penetrating."
—"That's . . . kind of the point. Want to try again?"
—"I think . . . um, no? It's too much pain."

—"Why don't I have lube?" Keiko's unsteady,
leaning on the wall. "Okay, instead
we'll do something else? Come on, get ready,
kneel down, you slut, and give me some head."
—"I don't know if I can, I'm maybe feeling
a bit too sick, or something, for kneeling."
—"Then I'll do you!" So Keiko sits down
on the toilet seat and Day goes to town
on her junk with her mouth, with vigor and ardor,
for quite a while, but no matter what
she does (and trust me, she does a lot)
Keiko's clit doesn't get any harder.
Which isn't essential, hardest ain't best,
but she's also looking increasingly distressed.

Finally, after the expiration
of a number of minutes (ten? fifteen?)
of awkwardly unilateral fellation,
Keiko shakes her head, twists from between
Day's lips, and begins jerkily rising.
Day looks at her like she finds this surprising.
—"What's up?" —"I'm sorry. I'm going. I'm done."
—"Was I doing it wrong? Aren't you having fun?"
Keiko starts a reply, but then she checks it.
She turns, and, leaving Day on her knees
she opens the door, looks back, then flees
through the club and out the exit
and off away through the sultry night,
down the street and out of sight.

Posted 30th October by @Eunuch_Onegin in series The Call-Out
content warnings: consequences
tags: transit; pajamas; rain; crying

everyone deals with consequences
(9/14)

But each night ends, of course, with dawning.
The sky goes pink then yellow then bright,
and Keiko awakes, stretching and yawning,
on a sofa-bed bathed in delicate light.
It's half past eight. The mattress is spiny
with uncoiling springs, and also tiny,
almost procrustean: her feet extend
a significant distance over the end.
She crawls out of bed, and goes looking
and finds some Folgers classic roast,
thoughtfully provided by the absent host,
and mutters to herself —"Well now we're cooking,"
and makes some coffee, and is going to pour
it out when she hears a key in the door.

Gaia bursts in, still attired
in last night's clothing, her makeup smeared:
—"Oh hi! Oh God, I'm so fucking wired,
I bought some coke, which just disappeared.
Is that coffee? Gimme! I'm craving.
Oh shit, I forgot: have I been behaving
badly? You were kind of emotional last night."
—"I was. I mean, I am. You're right . . .
but so, like what . . . what happened with Baker?"
—"Oh, would you believe, he's all top in the streets
but you get him in bed, he's a bottom in the sheets?
And a whiny bottom! More like Faker.
I left. I was all like, bye girl, bye.
And to think I'd been so obsessed with that guy!"

—"Wait, that's it? You haven't stopped talking
about him for months!" —"I know, what a bust!
All that plotting and cyber-stalking!
I guess I was carried away by lust.
But you can't trust boys. I shouldn't forget that!
And you're one of the people I've met that
I trust the most. But I'm not sure I get
what I've done that made you upset."
—"I maybe can't handle this conversation.
I'm sorry. I had a kind of intense
night last night, and I haven't made sense
of whatever happened. The situation
is just . . . I don't know what to say."
—"What's going on? Are you okay?"

—"Oh yeah, I'm fine. It's no big deal.
I had an encounter, okay, I kissed,
or maybe had sex, with Day, and I feel,
oh fuck, it's all so hard to untwist."
—"You hooked up with Day? That's very . . . exciting?"
—"It was weird. She was like, all groping and biting
and we went to the bathroom, and she seemed to think
she was gonna, like, fuck me over the sink,
but it hurt too much . . . I was so embarrassed . . .
then she went down on me for too long,
or perhaps it was me, I was doing it wrong . . ."
—"Keiko! You were sexually harassed!"
—"What? No I wasn't. It wasn't that bad."
—"Keiko, how much sex have you had?"

—"Well, not that much." —"Right, I suspected."
—"I slept with a cis girl once, or I tried.
It didn't work out . . ." —"You're so unprotected!
I know you think I tricked you or lied,
but if you're trans there's so much growing
up to do. We come out not knowing
the things that cis girls learn in their teens
about being a girl and what that means.
I'm maybe two or three years older
that you, but I've been out four years more.
I've been round the block. I know the score.
And also I'm like, not stronger, but . . . bolder?
Whatever. You're just so easy to hurt.
Which is why I didn't want us to flirt."

—"Well, but I mean, I think I'm learning,
Or how do I learn if I can't explore . . ."
—"Okay, I'm sorry you thought I was spurning
your advances that time. But the point is you're
a victim. Last night you were sexually assaulted,
and sexual abuse must immediately be halted
wherever it happens. We just can't let
abusers off, because if they get
away with it once, they continue abusing.
I'm here, as your friend, to offer support,
but also I really think that you ought
not to be forced into minimizing or excusing
what happened to you. You mustn't be weak."
Her eyes are shining. "You get to speak."

—"Okay, well it's nice you want to support me,
But I don't . . . I mean what do you want me to say?"
—"I'm a Dungeon Monitor. That's taught me
a lot about this. I'm sure there's a way
I can help, whether that means providing
an ear, or a voice. I'm so glad you're confiding
in me, that you told me what happened to you.
I hear you, I believe you. What you're saying is true."
—"But I'm not sure . . ." —"Don't worry, you'll question
yourself. Like, trauma makes you doubt.
You need to recover. I have a suggestion!
You can stay anonymous, and I'll put out
a call-out post. I know what to do.
I'll obtain restorative justice for you!"

Elsewhere, at this moment, I wake up feeling
very unusual. Do I feel . . . content?
But I'm also nervous, as if I'm stealing,
or living in a place where I can't make rent.
Kate wakes as well, and we pass some hours
wandering around among the towers,
in summer Philly, just the two of us.
We eat, we kiss, then we get the bus,
and then Kate goes home. There's no postponing
the matter any longer. As she goes inside
she's in a position where she has to decide
whether she will be concealing or owning
up to her actions. She doesn't balk.
—"Aashvi," she calls, "we need to talk."

—"What is it?" —"Okay, I have a confession.
I hooked up with someone. We didn't have sex,
but you know that I've been having depression,
and if this happened, then it all connects.
Of course in theory our relationship's poly
but this wasn't an impulsive act of folly,
or it was, but it came from a place of need."
Aashvi, who had been beginning to read
a detective novel, newly acquired,
while applying a face mask, and drinking a cup
of milky coffee, is curled up
on their modernist sofa, comfortably attired
in her pajamas. She stares, then blinks,
but doesn't reply. She stops. She thinks.

Some moments pass. The air's vibrating
with tension, or more to the point, it's not,
and Kate is clearly having trouble waiting.
—"You've gone all silent. Tell me! What?"
—"The way you're behaving is highly erratic.
You're engineering some kind of dramatic
confrontation between you and I.
You want a fight. So I'm wondering, why?"
—"Aashvi, fuck's sake, I mean like fucking
fuck, you know what the problem is here
but whenever I raise it you always steer
the conversation off, or find ways of ducking
the issue, or you find a way to make
it all about me. It's too much to take!"

—"Well, clearly you're not committed to maintaining
moderation here. Instead it appears
I am dismissive . . ." Kate's barely restraining
herself from sobs: visible tears
pour from her eyes, her cheeks glisten.
—"You're always judging and you never listen!
I don't want a baby! I think it's weird.
And being off hormones is worse than I feared,
and I can't say it because disagreeing
with you is scary. You're so smart and stern
you know all these things I'm supposed to learn,
and maybe you're perfect, but I can't keep being
totally absorbed in your perfect life,
as your social justice trophy wife!"

—"But we're not married." —"That's not the issue!
You're doing it again!" She can barely speak.
Aashvi proffers a box. —"Do you need a tissue?"
Kate takes it, wipes the tears from her cheek,
blows her nose —"I can't keep spending
my energy supporting you and blending
into your world. I can't invest
in cisness any more. I need a rest.
I don't have energy for educating
a cisgender kid. I need to be
in community with other people like me.
I'm trans, and I'm done with assimilating."
—"And yet you thought it quite alright
for me to invest in someone white?"

—"Okay, I'm wrong and bad and your virtue
is greater than mine. I'm glad that's clear."
—"Kate, what is this, how have I hurt you?"
—"You haven't, you're perfect and just and austere
and you don't have to pay me any attention.
If I'm being awkward some condescension
will shut me up. You don't have to care
that I'm so unhappy. Just say I'm unfair,
and point out the flaws in my argumentation,
and things can go on just like before."
—"Now Kate, enough! I won't endure
this barrage of unwarranted castigation.
This isn't okay. You can't just behave
in such a manner. It's very grave."

—"Well yeah, I realize you think I'm making
a fuss over nothing, but you know, I'm not."
—"Kate, what is this, are you breaking
up with me? Is that honestly what . . ."
—"No, I don't think we're like, ending,
or at least, I mean, I wasn't intending . . .
but I need to go back on hormones again,
I just can't survive without estrogen . . ."
—"But everything's planned! We're having a baby!"
—"We can put it on hold. I need some space.
I think I should maybe move out of this place
just for a while, to try it, then maybe
we can try again . . . oh I don't know,
but I'm going out. I've got to go."

—"Kate don't leave, you're making an error!"
But Kate's already begun her flight,
her bag in her hand. The look of terror
that Kate is wearing is quite a sight
(at least, in my imagination).
I don't think she expected this confrontation
to so decisively escalate.
Once she's outside the building, Kate
sends me a text, with a desperate appeal
to stay at mine. As I eagerly agree,
elsewhere, contemporaneously,
Day, unaware of the ordeal
she's about to be required to endure,
has just come through her apartment door.

Bette's inside, agitatedly pacing.
—"Oh Day, oh fuck me, what did you do?"
—"What do you mean?" Bette replies by embracing
her tightly, then asks —"Are they really true?"
—"Are what really true?" —"The accusations!
Oh my god, have you checked your notifications?"
—"Well no, my phone is out of juice."
—"You've been accused of sexual abuse!
—"By who?" —"Well look, by that girl, Gaia.
Wait, did she tag you? She didn't! That's low.
You're being accused and you don't even know."
—"We've barely met! She's a fucking liar."
—"No look, she says 'the victim preferred
to not be named.' She's just 'spreading the word.'"

—"Well who could it be? I mean it's Philly,
I fucked a couple of people I met,
so I don't, like, know. Like, this is silly!
How am I supposed . . . oh shit, I bet
it's this girl, Keiko who was like, obsessing
over Gaia, and you know, just stressing
out, and thinking she had no allure
because she liked a girl who didn't like her.
And like, I've been there, I know about hating
yourself, so I thought if we did some stuff
it would boost her confidence. I wasn't rough,
like all I was doing was demonstrating
she could be attractive, like, sexually.
You know, like the way you did with me."

—"Oh. My god. Are you, like, stupid?
I don't know how to even respond.
Your dick's not an arrow of fucking cupid
or some kind of dick-shaped magic wand.
You think you're some kind of sexual savior,
or that she'd be grateful for this behavior?
You can't fuck people because you think you should:
if desire's not selfish then desire's no good."
Day looks completely confused and dejected
like someone just kicked her when she thought she'd be fed.
She puts both her hands on top of her head.
—"This is all going wrong. I never expected . . .
so what do I do? Perhaps if I call
Keiko on the phone we can talk through it all?"

—"Day, I would really advise you not to."
—"But if we could just talk, she could hear my side,
we could sort this out. I mean I've got to
do something about this. I can't just hide.
I mean, like look, this post is claiming
I 'attacked her in a bathroom.' It's aiming
to make me sound like some rapist guy!
Why is she letting Gaia lie
about me like this? It's bad. It's vicious."
—"Day, it's natural that you're upset
but they're already suggesting that you're a threat.
It'll only make you look more suspicious
if you try to call her when she's made it clear
she doesn't want you anywhere near."

—"Well thanks for being sympathetic.
Jesus, Bette, I'm struggling here.
And I mean, I'd be apologetic . . .
oh wait, hold on, I have an idea!
What if you called up Keiko for me?
I understand that they could ignore me,
but everyone listens to what you say,
you can make this stop . . ." —"Uh-uh. No way."
—"You need to tell them, I never desired . . ."
—"You need to respect people's boundaries."
—"But Bette, I need you to help me, please!"
Bette suddenly looks extremely tired.
She sits on the sofa. —"This is too much stress.
Why is your life always such a mess?"

And one, and then the other, starts weeping,
whether from weariness or from pain.
After a humid summer of keeping
things held together, tears fall like rain,
which also, coincidentally, starts falling.
I'm closing my window when I hear Kate calling
up from the street: —"Hey let me in!
I walked from the subway. I'm soaked to the skin."
I gaze at her, as she stands waiting.
Around her feet raindrops burst,
small explosions, and a powerful thirst
appears in my body, as exhilarating
and uncontrolled as it is strange.
The weather is turning. Time for a change.

Posted 11th November by @Eunuch_Onegin in series The Call-Out
content warning: morality; world music
tags: Armageddon; carpentry; feminism; cheese

complications of a daytime date
(10/14)

Fortunate autumn. September rushes
over our heads. Migrating flocks
of warblers, jays, petrels, thrushes,
come, then leave. The equinox,
when the sun aligns with the equator,
passes. The dawns start coming later,
the sunsets sooner. The sudden rains
don't last for long. The heat remains:
that's global warming. Even the roses
are hanging on, this late in the year.
We know what's coming, the signs are clear,
whatever falls soon decomposes,
we know the world is in decay
but for now, it seems like a lovely day.

Kate's euphoric. She joyfully bounces
out of the subway, into the light.
—"I think it's positive," she announces,
"it's really a chance to get something right."
Kate's just agreed, which is why she's elated,
to lead this panel that is being created
for Day to be accountable to.
—"Or are you just flattered that Gaia asked you?"
—"Well, okay, I'm not denying
it's nice if I'm someone that people trust,
but also, if I can help, then I must."
—"Whatever," I say, "the world is dying,
We killed it, so do what you want. It's fine:
you have your pleasures, and I have mine."

I'm referring to the building we're about to enter:
the Morgan Library. Kate's never been,
and suspects it's immoral. —"We need to decenter
this view of the past as this kind of serene
procession of aristocratic 'cultures'
and remember that the rich are always vultures
feeding on the bodies of the dispossessed . . ."
—"Okay, but look! This place is the best."
It's three stories high. The ceiling is golden
and painted with copies from Raphael,
or someone like that, done pretty well.
There's a fireplace out of a castle in olden-
day Europa, and of course, there are books,
shelf upon shelf, wherever one looks.

I show Kate the way that, carefully hidden
behind a bookcase, a spiral stair,
provides the access to those forbidden
tiers of volumes, high in the air.
—"Okay," I say, "so grant your position
that there's something obscene about the condition
of being so rich that you can build
this stuff, but still, at least he fulfilled
well, I won't say, some kind of duty,
but some kind of vision. The world's unfair
and there's no justice anywhere,
but at least in places like this there's beauty.
He made us a refuge, a place to go.
There are worse things to do with that kind of dough."

—"Oh GOD!" Kate replies, extremely loudly.
Numerous bystanders turn and stare.
I give her a look. She laughs proudly.
"You're such an aesthete. Do you really care
that much about art, that you make excuses
for the exploitation which produces
this stuff? I think we have to believe
in justice as something we can achieve."
I laugh myself —"And good will prevail?"
Are we, I wonder, getting in a fight?
I know I should stop, but I can't: I'm right.
"Movements for justice necessarily fail.
You can't fight power unless you're strong
But then you're in power, and you're what's wrong."

—"That's such a fatalistic perspective . . ."
—"That power corrupts? Seems clearly true."
—"Like, power's not the only objective,
there are other kinds of things you can do . . .
I know you'll accuse me of separatism,
But I think that radical feminism,
it's not just transphobes buying farms,
these were women responding to the actual harms
they faced, and it's part of a wider tradition
or asking, like, how do you build outside
of abusive structures. Separatism can provide
one way of working towards abolition."
—"So you think we can learn from Charlotte Bunch
or Mary Daly? You're out to lunch!"

—"Okay, well yes, I've been re-reading
Mary Daly . . ." —"I know! I saw
the book by the bed!" —". . . and fine, conceding
of course she hates us, there's also more
to it than that. She gets that oppression
is material, that violence and dispossession,
are all about bodies, it's just she can't see
we're women as well, materially."
—"Kate, what is this, this is alarming.
Aren't you the one who's like 'fuck cis queers'?
So why would you care about their ideas?
This is like cutting, it's like you're self-harming!"
—"Well my relation to transness is very much like
Daly's relation to being a dyke . . ."

—"That's not the point! Like, this is madness!"
—"That's kind of an ableist thing to say."
And I look in her eyes, and I see sadness
where before she'd been so joyous and gay.
—"Alright," I breathe out, "Let's stop debating.
I'm sorry, okay, I'm de-escalating.
I realize I may have been a bit mean."
—"Yeah, you were." —"Okay, have you seen
these?" And I show her the illuminated
books of hours, and the autograph
Brontë poems. She sees a staff
member and asks if he's compensated
fairly. He says he'd rather not say.
We adjourn to the Starbucks across the way.

We buy our coffees and find some seating.
Kate's gone in one of her quiet moods.
I get the impression she's avoiding meeting
my eyes. The sudden vicissitudes
of others' emotions are things I'm sorely
unprepared for. I handle them poorly.
—"Hey Kate, will you look me in the eyes.
Please, come on, I'll apologize,
I promise. Just will you please engage me?"
—"I'm not not engaging. I just feel ill.
I've got a headache. So please, can you chill?"
—"I'm sorry, it's just, it tends to enrage me,
this silent treatment. If we're in a fight,
we need to talk about it, alright?"

—"Okay, what is it you have this burning
need to discuss?" —"Okay, I'll admit
I think this whole panel is very concerning,
I'm unhappy you're getting involved in it.
I mean, so there's this accusation
but you haven't conducted an investigation
you don't know what happened, or even to who,
or whether this accusation is even true!"
—"Do you really think a person would make it
if it wasn't? I mean, for what? For fun?
Come on, this is feminism 101."
—"It's not that I think someone would fake it
it's just, it's hard, but if both those involved
are trans, is it really that easily resolved?"

—"You mean, if there isn't a clearly lopsided
power imbalance? But we have to face
the material factors by which we're divided,
like class, and age, and clout and race.
Day's super visible, people know her,
she's always inviting people to blow her
on Twitter, and posting about being non-op.
She has a brand. She's like, power top.
And she's white, she has money. I might be frightened
of her, if I was young, or poor."
—"There are power differences between us, sure,
but whatever, also, it ain't enlightened
to suggest trans women are a sexual threat.
I dunno, this discourse just makes me fret."

—"Well okay, I agree. I mean, ideally
a justice system shouldn't blame, or shun,
but help the person to admit freely
that they're responsible for hurting someone.
That's really the only way anyone heals:
I mean, with my rapist, if he knew how it feels
to be raped, if he really, deep in his heart
understood what he did, that could be the start
of healing for us both. Of restoration."
—"Oh Kate, you're so good. And you know, of course
that would be lovely. But you simply can't force
people to repent, or make expiation.
If we build our own system, we'll just replicate
the defense of order we all say we hate."

—"The idea that justice is just a fiction
is copaganda! It makes us submit
to the cops, and to the jurisdiction
of the courts, instead of fighting it."
—"Yeah well, I wish I could be persuaded.
These kids won't find any justice unaided,
but what kind of justice do you think you can give?
Accountability? It's punitive!
I know I'm against the spirit of the times,
but what's at issue here is a relationship
and I think it's really a dangerous slip
to start seeing that in terms of crimes.
I preferred it the way it used to be,
before queerness discovered morality.

—"I feel like recently, claims to virtue
have become the way you win a fight.
Like I'm totally licensed to hate or hurt you
if I first establish, I'm in the right."
—"Come on, that's bullshit. You're misconstruing
everything I say. What we're doing
isn't punishment, it's about being there
for your sisters, about the duty of care
we have for each other. It's about relying
on other trans women, and you know, I thought
I'd be able to turn to you for support.
Like, can't you help me? I'm here, I'm trying
to do something good." —"Okay, that's true.
But that goodness might be misguiding you."

—"Well if not goodness, what should I be guided
by, do you think?" —"Well what about us?
Not that I need your undivided
attention, or for you to like, make a fuss
of me, but we're new, and it's kind of exciting,
and instead, you're obsessed with these children fighting."
—"It isn't fighting. And shut up, there's no need
for you to be jealous. I'm feeling freed.
It's not zero-sum. I finally ended
things with Aashvi, who was such a rock
she became a burden, and like, it's a shock,
But it's like I finally comprehended
that I have all this energy. I feel so light."
—"That's good," I lean back. "Perhaps you're right."

Why do I say this? The truth is, reader
I've gone and fallen in love with Kate.
I can't upset her too much. I need her.
And also she isn't wrong: she's great!
She's has such passion, such hope, she's so dashing,
her hands waving, her eyes flashing,
her little jumps in her seat, the way
she pulls at her hair when she wants to say
something, but is letting me finish speaking,
this gesture of barely managed restraint:
she's crazy, but there's nothing about her faint
or listless. And so I'm kind of freaking
out, and realizing if I want to defuse
this argument, then I have to lose.

Kate says —"You can help me, we'll do this together . . ."
—"Listen," I say, "this is all a lot.
Let's go for a walk. It's gorgeous weather,
warm but not unbearably hot.
Plus I swear, since we've been seated
this is the seventh time they've repeated
that same bloody Ibeyi song.
Which means it's a fact: we've been here too long."
Kate laughs, and I think okay I'm succeeding!
and basically drag her out through the door.
"How about a joke? Okay, Niels Bohr,
a cop pulls him over because he's speeding
and asks, 'Do you know you were going too fast?'
He says, 'No. But I know where I am at last!'"

Kate doesn't get it, so I start outlining
quantum theory, and uncertainty:
"It's the physics version of not defining
that which has a history . . ."
—"We've gone from Niels Bohr to Nietzsche!"
She laughs again. "You're such a teacher!"
—"I wish! I got my PhD
in Early Modern poetry!
Imagine thinking I had the potential
to get hired without doing something queer,
or dating to earlier than, like, last year.
If I'd stuck to the experiential
I wouldn't be working in a fucking shop!"
—"Yeah, well I'm freelance! You want to swap?"

—"So now we're competing over whose position
is most precarious?" —"We are! Hell yeah!
That's trans girl culture! It's the trans condition."
—"Well it's good to know there's something we share."
We laugh, and this isn't commiseration.
but instead a kind of celebration:
we stand together against the cis!
At Twentieth and Park we stop and kiss
and I buy her a single perfect flower
from a guy outside a health-food shop
Kate says —"I could almost punch a cop!
When we're together we have so much power."
At Twelfth, I realize where we are.
—"Oh Kate, we're almost at Giant Bar!"

—"What's that?" —"Okay, the name's misleading,
the place is tiny, I mean really small.
It's the only bar in this whole bleeding
country I actually like at all.
It's not a pub, but it's a consolation."
—"It's a little early for inebriation . . ."
—"No! If anything, it's already too late.
I mean, this is supposed to be a date!
And we went for coffee! What a blunder!"
I take her hand, and together we flit
through East Village streets obliquely lit
by the unseasonal sun, as it's sinking under
the tops of the towers we're leaving behind:
our footsteps matching, our fingers entwined.

When we get there, the bar's still quiet.
I order Campari with a little squeeze
of orange, and Kate has whisky and diet.
The gay bartender has put out cheese
thoughtfully cut up, on a little platter,
(these little touches really matter)
and Prince and Lisa are duetting on "Head."
—"You were just a virgin on your way to be wed,"
I sing to Kate, and we both start dancing.
—"And then I came on your wedding gown!"
I conclude, and giggling, we settle down
and begin to get tipsy. The fall is advancing
remorselessly outside, but within this banquette,
at least for an evening, we're able to forget.

Posted 21st December by @Eunuch_Onegin in series The Call-Out
content warnings: pedagogy
tags: doors; axes; herbal teas

on taking control of one's own fate
(11/14)

And now rewind: the leaves are rising
softly through the air, to reattach
to the trees, and resume photosynthesizing;
the russet turning, patch by patch
back to green, as if by magic.
It's comic, as in, the opposite of tragic,
but of course it's nothing but a poet's trick:
all I have is words, I can't unpick
the seconds, or reverse the direction
of flow of heat, to less from more,
as prescribed so clearly by the second law
of thermodynamics. Through the selection
and ordering of narrative,
I can give the effect, but that's all I can give.

So backwards! It's September, and Keiko's returning
to uni for her second academic year
in pursuit of that special kind of learning
that leaves you incapable of having a career
as anything other than that magical creature:
an artist. Her college has the feature
of combining courses in making art
with others that claim to be able to impart
not skill, but wisdom, and to offer instruction
in analysis and critical thought.
This term she's signed up for a course that is taught
(in accordance with proper dramatic construction)
by Aashvi! If you're thinking this world is small
you've no understanding of fate at all.

As we've gathered, Keiko's predispositions,
aesthetically, are conservative,
but "Decolonial Apparitions"
(as the course is titled) seems to give
her something to chew on. I'm not pretending
I get it, but it presently results in her sending
an email to Aashvi, asking to speak
during office hours, maybe next week,
about the essay on which she's working.
Aashvi has to say yes: it's how she gets paid,
and so, daunted but undismayed
Keiko arrives and begins lurking
more than twenty minutes before
the appointed time, by the office door.

When the bing of the elevator
puts an end to Keiko's wait
it's almost a full hour later.
—"Oh yes, it's you. Sorry I'm late."
Has Aashvi been crying? Her eyes are bleary.
"Come in, sit down. Now what was your query?"
Keiko sits. Her chair goes creeeeeak.
—"I read, um, 'Can the Subaltern Speak?'
And I mean, why can't she? It's sort of confusing . . ."
She stops, from embarrassment or fear
then plunges on, "I'm trans, I'm queer,
I'm sort of subaltern, I guess, if you're using
that term, and I make art, or try . . .
Like, can't I speak? Or if not, why?"

Aashvi sighs. —"She's not preventing
the subaltern from speaking. She cannot be heard
because the statement she is representing
appears, in dominant discourse, absurd.
One is not subaltern, by definition,
if one can pay for college tuition!
So of course you can speak. But perhaps you can say
only certain things, in a certain way,
because you are both somewhat located,
precisely by 'trans' and terms like these,
in hegemonic hierarchies,
and also somewhat alienated.
In so far as the marginal is expressed in art
the culture is prone to ignore that part."

—"Okay! That helps! Like I have been feeling
I mean, like you're saying, that people ignore
like half what I say, and perhaps that's revealing,
maybe it's about, I don't know, I'm not sure,
but maybe it's about . . . like racism maybe?
Some people treat me like I'm a baby,
who needs someone else to speak for me!
And I read that that's supposed to be
like an Asian stereotype? Infantilization?"
—"I think it can be a mistake to read
theory from a place of personal need.
Which isn't to say that your frustration,
isn't real, or that these things aren't true,
but this text is not a text about you.

—"It is not self-help. Her work's pursuing
a critique of a certain theoretical trend."
—"Okay, but in theory, if someone is doing
something like this, and they're, like, a friend,
but also they're privileged, I guess, or whatever,
is that a relationship you just have to sever?"
—"I cannot provide you pastoral advice.
Perhaps your friend is not very nice,
but privilege is not a psychological condition.
Are white people racist? I mean, of course!
But this is beating a very dead horse:
it only describes their structural position.
It's as if one went out of one's way to insist
the bourgeoisie are capitalist!"

—"It's structural. Okay, I get that,
but what do I do if reading this text
made me . . . angry, or like upset that . . ."
—"Anger is natural. I am often vexed.
But if we are righteous we stop critiquing
the terms through which we are even speaking.
Spivak describes 'the impossible no'
of deconstruction. One cannot go
outside of discourse, one is always complicit.
One need not put up with people's crap,
of course, but innocence is also a trap.
One must use one's guilt, and not dismiss it.
For an artist, it's a duty one must not shirk.
Now is that all? I have to work."

Keiko stands and leaves slowly,
floats out the building, takes the train,
with a distant expression, as if she's wholly
absorbed by events inside her brain.
Occasional emotions—distress? irritation?—
cross her features. Internal conversation
manifests in her sometimes moving her lips
or scowling. She bumps into people, trips
on steps, almost misses her connection,
but makes it home. The next few days
she wanders around in a kind of haze.
One morning, she's been staring at her own reflection
in the mirror for fifteen minutes straight
when Gaia calls. —"It's a yes from Kate!"

—"Wait. Who's Kate? What's she agreeing?"
—"Journalist Kate! She's said she'll be
part of the group that's overseeing
the meetings for accountability."
—"Oh yeah. Is that good?" —"It is! She's for real.
Everyone respects her. I think she's ideal.
She gets consent, which of course a lot
of older trans women just do not."
—"Gaia, this process, it's set up so that . . .
I kept away from the whole thing online,
like you said I should, and that was fine,
I guess, but I'm asking, do people know that
it's me? Like some of them must know?"
—"Well some, for sure. But the number is low."

—"Well is that okay? Like, this is about me.
It's a problem of mine that's meant to be solved.
Maybe this shouldn't happen without me?
I think I need to be more involved."
—"What do you mean? I've kept you updated,
and I definitely don't think you're obligated
to stand up in public and share your pain."
—"You're right, I know . . . It's hard to explain!
I just. I just think I need to make choices.
This feels like it's got a life of its own,
or you're off doing it, and I'm alone
away to the side, not one of the voices
in which the community's interested:
just some sort of helpless little kid."

Gaia's voice takes on a tremulous inflection.
—"Keiko, are you . . . are we okay?
You know I have a lot of affection . . .
I'm such a fuck-up! I get carried away,
I'm always trying to do things faster,
and then it's always a disaster,
I'm sorry. But listen, I can make this right,
come to the meeting next Wednesday night,
like, not with Day, just preparation,
you should come, and discuss what you want to be
the outcome, and then you'll have agency,
we'll just be helping with implementation."
And Keiko must still be totally gay
for Gaia, because she replies: —"Okay."

And so it comes to pass, one gloomy
Wednesday in October, they gather to meet
at my apartment. It isn't roomy,
so I go to the bar just down the street.
Truthfully, Kate and I have been fighting,
again. I don't really like her inviting
this into our home, but we meet halfway:
the meeting will happen, but I won't stay.
As I slip through the building doorway
I see Gaia and Keiko down the block.
Keiko's saying —"Well yeah, it's a shock,
I know we've been doing this process your way,
but you should have told me, right from the start,
that you had Baker taking part."

They go inside, still debating.
Of course, Gaia has made them late,
so the other three are already waiting,
sat on my sofa. There's Baker, there's Kate
and there's Janet (remember? who does the cooking
at the picnics). The last of these three is looking
typically grumpy, and wearing a hat
indoors. When Gaia comes into the flat
Janet reacts like she bit something sour.
—"Oh hi, so glad you joined us at last."
—"Sorry, queer time. We came as fast . . ."
—"Well. We've been here for half an hour.
I came because it's the right thing to do,
but I didn't realize I'd be waiting on you."

—"Dudes," says Baker, "come on, like, chill it."
—"Now," says Kate, "this isn't a race.
The session this evening continues until it
gets everybody involved to a place
they're good with. Keiko, I'm glad you got here,
and clearly, Day, your abuser, is not here.
We're here to support you. For us to succeed
it would help if you'd talk about what you might need."
—"Um," says Keiko, "I guess I've been dealing
alright, and it's nice to be offered support.
I suppose I haven't given it much thought . . ."
Gaia jumps in. —"It should be about healing,
like that's the purpose. I think that we
are here to heal the community."

Kate gives her a look, but she doesn't see it,
her eyes are down. "So we ought to begin
by discussing community. How do we be it,
or what's the relation we want to be in?
Clearly, some versions are destructive:
oppressive, fascist. If they're seductive
it's because they offer a place to belong
and insist that unity will make us strong.
Now the *fasces* is a symbol that was appropriated
from the Romans: it's sticks that are tied round an axe,
like stronger together. But the artefacts
archaeologists find, the oldest dated
have an axe of a very particular kind:
actually, it's a *labrys* they find."

—"Where is this going?" Kate enquires.
—"Somewhere, I promise! Bear with me.
Before the Roman or Greek empires
invented colonial masculinity,
this *labrys* belonged to a mother deity
who bound us in love, not homogeneity.
Virtue's from *vir*, meaning a man
but centering the feminine means that we can
work for goodness without relying
on structures in which we punish and shun.
Justice means helping everyone!
We shouldn't aim at identifying
mere redress. As queers, our goal
is to learn to remake the culture as a whole!"

At last she looks up, like in expectation,
but no-one has anything much to say.
There's a risky gap in the conversation.
Then Keiko fills it. —"But what about Day?"
(as she says it, her body visibly tenses)
"Don't her actions have consequences?
What happens to her, and to me as well?
The last two months have been like hell.
I can't go to sleep, I keep reliving
what happened, trying to figure out
my feelings, but all I feel is doubt.
Should I just forget it, or try forgiving?
What did she do? Was it really that bad?
What's wrong with me? Why am I sad?

"Like fuck you, Gaia, and your grand ambition,
actually. You're always stuck in your head,
you're always giving some disquisition,
what about listening to me instead?
You say you're my friend! But you're such a liar,
you never think about what I desire,
it's like you're unable to hear my voice . . .
You made me do this. I had no choice.
This is all just more of your selfish behavior.
All you care about's some big idea.
Do you even know I'm sitting right here?
You make these promises, like some kind of savior,
but I'm in pain, and all you do
is make the whole thing all about you!"

Gaia flinches, and starts emitting
a high-pitched animal keening yelp,
then clenches her fists, and commences hitting
herself in the face. —"I was trying to help!"
she shrieks, "That was all, I was only trying . . ."
then she runs to the door, and goes flying
out of the apartment, and down the stairs.
Keiko crumples into one of the chairs,
weeping. Kate goes over, and, kneeling
down by her side, touches her arm.
—"Okay," she says, "we're keeping calm.
You're safe. It's over. As you said, you're dealing
with a lot right now. And if we can do . . ."
—"But why couldn't she just like me too?"

—"I'm sorry, what?" But Keiko's crying
so intensely now, with such little restraint
that she's barely capable of replying.
At last, she manages to produce a faint
—"It doesn't matter. I'm such a loser."
—"You're not. I promise. Perhaps you could use a
warming cup of herbal tea."
—"Why are you being so nice to me?"
Kate goes over to start the kettle.
—"Well something just happened, it's clear you're in pain.
I'll make you tea, and you can explain
what's going on, and we can settle
on a plan." She smiles. Outside in the street
the wind starts howling, the rain becomes sleet.

Posted 4th January by @Eunuch_Onegin in series The Call-Out
creator chose not to give content warnings
tags: zines; phalluses; heterosexuals dying

a discussion regarding various offenses
(12/14)

No more tricks. Let's just keep moving.
October continues. Everything gets worse.
Nothing shows any signs of improving,
neither the weather, nor my verse.
There's no more beauty. Okay, admitted,
there are days when the shifting clouds are slitted
with sudden sun, which falls in strips
across the buildings, and dazzles and skips
from off the windows, at last denuded
of air conditioners. Days which might
seem made of breezes and dancing light,
but that's just appearance. Don't be deluded.
The moving finger, or whatever, has writ.
It's settled. Everything's going to shit.

Day's state of dismay and desperation
gets more intense as October goes on,
then November starts with a communication
from Kate, explaining that Gaia's gone,
and she's in charge, and naming plenty
of texts, from Brownmiller through Valenti,
Day ought to study, in order to prepare
for the group's first meeting. "It's so unfair!"
Day mutters to herself, reading the email.
She goes to find Bette. —"Oh my God, I'm pissed.
Look! They've set me a reading list!
Like what the fuck? 'Visions of Female
Sexual Power'? I'm a woman too!
This is such bullshit. What should I do?"

Bette looks round slowly. She's comfortably lying
stretched out on the sofa, vaping weed
and watching a movie about rich guys dying
on Everest, because they refuse to heed
their Sherpa's eminently sensible warning
that they're setting out too late in the morning.
She frowns and pauses. —"Okay, let me see."
She reads. "So, what don't you agree
should be on this list? It seems, like, normal.
A bit white feminist, but she has that zine
about sex and race in the anarchist scene . . .
It's mostly pretty standard for a formal
process like this." She pauses and vapes.
—"Standard? This stuff is all about rapes!"

—"Well, rape, consent, assault, and power . . ."
—"But that's not me. It's just not true.
I'm not a rapist, and I won't allow a
fucking 'panel' of fuck knows who
to say I am. I have to fight it.
I'm gonna reply. Will you help me write it?
Are you on their side?" —"I'm not on their side,
Day. Like, Jesus, all I've done is tried
to support you since this shitshow started.
Don't turn on me. You have to allow
this thing to happen. Can't stop it now.
That ship has sailed. It's gone. Departed.
Just read the books. It's all you can do.
You might even learn a thing or two."

—"Oh Bette, fuck off." —"Well maybe learning
more about feminism will help you find
the energy to follow through on returning
to school." —"Oh stop! Or please be kind?
My life is under, like, demolition."
—"And why do you think you're in this position?
Have you stopped to ask, like, 'why the fuck
is this happening to me?'" —"It's just bad luck!
Like, maybe ask Gaia what was her reason
for dragging me? Ask her why did she get
her little friends on the internet
to fucking declare it open season.
Why'd they all line up to say
'me too, I was also abused by Day'?"

—"So let me get this straight: you're claiming
it's nothing to do with anything you've done
and all these people are just defaming
you on Twitter, for why, for fun?
Like Day, you know it takes two to tango.
I won't disagree those bitches can go
love themselves, they're drama queens,
but don't you deny this also means
you've been doing something incorrectly.
Like, take responsibility!
You're failing at non-monogamy
and generally life, kind of abjectly.
You know, when we met I thought I'd found
an adult, at last. Did I get clowned!"

—"But you were always making fun of
me for my job, or wanting to commit.
Sleeping around was actually one of
the things I did for your benefit!
You're being really arbitrary!"
—"Okay, well I teased you because it was scary.
You seemed to have your life all set
and my job is jerking it on the internet,
so I needed something where I was stronger
and that was sex and getting high.
But it turns out your life was all a lie.
You just hung on for like, way longer
to male privilege. You were so afraid
to leave that life, you just fucking stayed."

—"Well I've left it now! That's all surrendered."
—"And now your life is a trash-heap too!
You're not, like, better at being transgendered,
I'm garbage, and still I'm better than you.
You lost your job, you alienated
seems like, half the girls you dated,
you're accused of assaulting a POC . . .
Trannies are our only community.
Cis people suck, and chasers can't be trusted,
they're all fucking cowards. You can make them pay
to fuck you, but after, they're not gonna stay.
Trannies are it. Without them you're busted.
If you don't do this, if you don't make amends,
you're just not gonna have any friends."

Day scowls, and snaps —"But they're persecuting . . ."
and the fight goes on, but it's clear Bette's right,
so after an hour of fruitless disputing,
and a week of reading, on the appointed night,
Day drags herself across the city
to stand before the appointed committee
way up in Ridgewood, at my place.
She comes through the door, with a look on her face
that screams, I want to get this ordeal
over and done with. Which isn't smart.
She might be holding defiance in her heart
but if I were her I'd try to conceal
that fact. She stares with a visible sneer
right in Kate's eyes, and announces —"I'm here."

—"Welcome! I want to begin these discussions
by talking about how our actions incur
certain consequences and repercussions"
(Kate's doing that thing where she acts all mature)
"for us and for others. Just by appearing
you show that you're committed to hearing
useful critique. So I'm really impressed
you're here. You should know we all want the best
for you, but in order to get that it's vital
we account for some actions which we'll have to name,
not because we want to punish or shame,
we're not the police, we don't want a recital
of guilt, but because we can help you reflect
on how you treat others, and on how to respect . . ."

Janet jumps in. —"You're just very aggressive.
I mean, I've seen the way you flirt
with people on Twitter, and I think it's oppressive.
I'm not surprised to hear you hurt
people in life. Any conversation
you join, it's always the sexualization.
And don't get me started on the pictures you post!
I'm not the only one who's grossed
out by suddenly seeing an erection
under a skirt, but very on view,
out of nowhere, out of the blue
in the middle of a freaking comments section!
A survivor might see it, or someone below
the age of consent. How would you know?"

Kate tries to stop this, —"Please, can we dial . . ."
but Day has already started to speak:
—"Oh right, so now my body's on trial?
I thought this was supposed to be 'useful critique'?
Like, sorry, not sorry, the free expression
of trans sexuality isn't aggression
and none of you bitches can make me stop.
I'm proud of my body, I'm proud I'm non-op,
and I think it's good to share that feeling.
I won't be shamed, or go back in my box
because you freak out at the sight of cocks,
and never learnt the tools for dealing
with internalized transmisogyny.
That's your problem. Don't put it on me."

Now Baker joins in —"Hey wow, now hold it,
for sure, like, be sex positive,
but you gotta hear a no when you're told it.
Like, women aren't always able to give
clear expression, because socialization,
and you know, like, sex objectification . . ."
—"That's very helpful, could you please explain:
what's it like to be a girl again?
I think I need a man's perspective."
—"Day," says Janet, "that's very rude.
We want what's best, but your attitude . . ."
—"You want what's best? No, your objective
is to ruin my life. I can't win this fight.
You're Gaia's buddies, and you think she's right."

—"Everyone, please have some moderation!"
Kate shouts. The voices fall away.
"Gaia's not involved in this conversation,
and no-one's conspiring against you, Day,
I promise." She gives her a friendly smile.
"I can see you feel like this is a trial
but Keiko doesn't want that, and neither do I.
I want to talk. Do you think you could try?"
Day scowls. —"Okay." —"We're here to support that,"
Kate smiles again, "and help you succeed.
So I sent you a list of books to read . . ."
—"I read Brownmiller. And actually I thought that
it kind of sucked." —"Well, that's okay.
Can I ask you why you felt that way?"

—"Well, it says that rape is a tool for attacking
women, and that you shouldn't trust
anyone, basically, who isn't lacking
a penis, and to me that just . . .
sounds really terfy, and kind of reductive."
—"You don't have to rape to be destructive."
—"Okay, but whatever you've think that I've done
no one is saying I raped anyone."
—"Her point is that rape is a material condition
for the perpetuation of patriarchy . . ."
—"But what's that got to do with me?
Like I'm a woman." —"But your position
or mine" (Kate sounds a little annoyed)
"is in this context. We're not in a void."

—"Well also it's racist." —"Well, estimated
by the standards of now, then yeah, I admit
the stuff on Emmett Till is dated . . ."
—"It's racist!' —"Okay, yes fine, a bit,
but other texts on the list are injecting
a consideration of intersecting
identities, and there are still some things
a radical feminist analysis brings,
you know, as context, that are really . . . real.
Sex isn't just pleasure. It's a means to extract
labor from women, by producing the 'fact'
of gender. So Brownmiller helps to reveal
the material basis that men want hid.
I mean, whatever exactly you did . . ."

—"Whatever exactly? Wait, do you really . . .
do you not even know my alleged, like, 'crime'?"
—"Well, not in detail. I mean, so, clearly
to heal survivors need space and time,
and often demanding a survivor perform a
'narrative' just makes her relive her trauma."
—"No wait, no wait, so like, just now
all this stuff on the material basis of how
sex like, functions, or whatever you're saying . . .
you don't even know what you're talking about!"
—"Well that's where theory can help us out . . ."
—"This is my life! This isn't playing!
Like, what do you think you're here to do?
You're not even trying to find out what's true!"

—"This isn't a court. This is harm reduction.
The point is there's stuff you all need to know,
political stuff, and I'm giving instruction
to try and help this community grow."
—"Well you aren't helping!" —"Well fuck, I'm trying!
You're all so needy, you're basically crying
out for my help . . ." —"Bullshit! Who died
and made you the boss who gets to decide
what people's needs are? It's like you're feeding
on whatever happened with Keiko and me,
and Gaia, I guess, so you get to be
wise, and central, and like, a leading
community member. So you get to belong.
That's really gross and selfish and wrong."

Kate's silent, like she can't accept she heard that,
and Day is as well, like she can't believe
she could have come up with a single word that
came out of her mouth. —"I'm going to leave,"
says Janet. "This blows. Baker, you coming?"
—"Oh well, I don't know. This is kind of bumming
me out." —"We don't have to sit and take
being talked to this way. She can jump in a lake.
It's not worth the effort. Come on, I'm walking."
Baker pauses. —"Guys like me
who are also injured by patriarchy,
we hear you, Kate, like, when you're talking.
And Day, grow up. I'm gonna head.
Peace. I think this process is dead."

Kate looks at Day. —"Did you really mean that?"
—"I'm sorry. Maybe I went too far."
—"I mean, I get it, you know, I've been that
recently-out fuck-up you are.
Accepting help is terrifying . . ."
—"You're not, like, helping! God! Stop lying!"
Kate squeezes her nose. —"Alright, no more.
You don't want to listen, so what's this for?
I don't need this . . . well, this rejection.
Just, try to be kinder? Now go. Just go."
So Day takes off, into the blow
and bluster outside. Kate, in dejection,
stays there, sitting apparently sunk
in thought, 'til midnight, when I get home drunk.

—"Hello my darling," I say as I wobble
unsteadily in, "I had a good night!
And listen, I'm sorry about our squabble.
I'll try to support you more, alright?
I ran into a bunch of trannies,
Otter, Juno, both of the Annies,
so I got a bit tipsy. But it was fun!
So how was your thingy? Is everything done?"
She doesn't answer. "Are you sleeping?
Love?" More silence. "Are you okay?"
Finally she says —"Just go away,"
and then she begins loudly weeping.
There's a roll of thunder. Rain starts to fall.
I hug her. She sobs, "I failed them all!"

Posted 7th February by @Eunuch_Onegin in series The Call-Out
creator chose not to give content warnings
tags: planets; blizzards; gin; jets

some episodes of lateral strife
(13/14)

Despite our creation of an ozone hole a
number of million miles square
winter still comes. At the pole the polar
vortex cycles the bitter air,
then shifts, because the jet stream is slower
now, to chill the cities of the lower
latitudes. You can see your breath.
The news says the homeless might freeze to death.
Cars stop starting. Pipes start breaking.
Landlords turn down their tenants' heat
to try to force them into the street
and raise the rent. It's all about making
the best of your opportunities,
when the mercury's down to five degrees.

Elsewhere a shining plane is taking
off from smoggy Los Angeles,
traversing the cold front, bumping and shaking,
and descending into the northern freeze.
Gaia's on board. She took a vacation,
as in, she vacated her situation.
She stayed with friends, got laid a bunch,
walked on the beach, went out for lunch
at Mexican restaurants, started drinking
in the afternoon, then continued at night,
kept on insisting she was going to write,
but didn't, and generally avoided thinking
about what happened. But it couldn't last.
She's coming home, and she's travelling fast.

Within a week she's able to wangle
a job in a café extremely near
to Keiko's uni. What's her angle?
Is she hoping that Keiko might appear?
Or is this proximity adventitious?
Whichever it is, in expeditious
fashion Keiko walks into the place
and finds herself staring Gaia in the face.
Her first response is, weirdly, laughter.
—"Oh fuck the world. Uh-uh. No.
Not today." She turns to go.
Gaia leaves the till and comes running after.
—"Please can we talk? I think I can take
half an hour. I'm due a break."

Keiko's hand is gripping the handle,
but it's freezing outside. —"I'll get you a drink.
I just want to talk, I won't cause a scandal.
I've had some time, you know, to think."
—"Okay, but I want an espresso cortado.
And a sandwich. Egg and avocado."
Gaia smiles. —"I'll bring them now."
She does. Then she says, —"I've been thinking how
it all went wrong, how much I upset you.
I'm really sorry. It makes me sad
that I set on fire the friendship we had,
or more than friendship. I can't forget you.
I've been reflecting, and I think you're great,
and I want to ask you, like, out on a date."

Whatever Keiko might have been expecting,
it isn't this. She jolts her head
like she's been slapped —"You've been reflecting?
You just want to keep me on a thread!
You cannot bear if I don't come running
whenever you call. Oh God, you're cunning.
Or maybe you actually believe this shit.
Whatever, I'm tired of being gaslit.
I read this essay about how whiteness
makes white trans women think they can treat
trans women of color like pieces of meat.
You're all so convinced of your own rightness
and oppression, or whatever. I don't know if it's true
of all white trannies, but it sounded like you."

Now, Gaia isn't the best at grasping
actual refusal, but it seems like she tries.
She sits for a while clasping and unclasping
her hands, then looks in Keiko's eyes.
—"I'm sorry I'm white, and I know I messed up,
but come on Keiko, I've totally 'fessed up.
I've said I'm sorry. I get carried away
and that's what happened with this thing with Day.
I think that maybe I might be autistic
or else I maybe have ADHD.
Like being careful is hard for me.
I'm trying to be less . . . optimistic,
but that isn't cunning. That's like, my brain.
How can I make you trust me again?"

—"I don't think you can, after what transpired.
And also it's not . . . like, trust? That's weird.
I didn't trust you. I loved. I desired,
but what you are isn't how you appeared.
I guess I learned a lot from knowing
you for a while. Okay, I'm going.
Thanks for the coffee." She gets up to leave.
Gaia reaches out and grabs her sleeve,
—"That can't be it! We have a connection!"
—"Gaia, a connection has to go two ways.
You only liked me when I gave you praise.
What you want from me is your own reflection."
—"But I'm not like that! Not anymore!"
But Keiko's already out of the door.

And so are we. Through the magic
of the written word, we can blink our eyes
and a totally different, but equally tragic
scene can appear. As regards the demise
in a storm of online recrimination
of the process for Day's rehabilitation,
Bette's been, well, let's say, not amused.
Since the start of December she's simply refused
to talk to Day. Even though they're sleeping
in a bed together, she just won't speak.
The stand-off is now in its second week.
So, scene: their apartment. Day is weeping,
or at least lamenting, stretched out on the floor,
which makes her really quite hard to ignore.

Bette's doing her best. She's looking stoic,
sitting on the sofa, and trying to eat
a bowl of ramen. It's almost heroic
how she acts like there isn't a girl at her feet,
demanding attention. Call her uncaring,
but you have to admire her poise and her bearing.
—"Bette," Day wails, "what will it take?
Just fucking answer for fuck's fucking sake!"
And then, in a moment of inspiration,
she gets to her knees, reaches out,
and spills Bette's ramen. Bette gives a shout,
and jumps to her feet, all indignation.
—"That burns! It's hot! What's wrong with you?"
but Day is grinning. At last, she's got through.

—"Oh! You answered! Oh my God! I made you!"
—"Because you attacked me! That fucking hurt."
—"Oh my god, we're talking. I was really afraid you
would never answer." —"You ruined my skirt!"
—"What could I do? You were just so silent."
—"I dunno, how about, not be violent?"
—"But Bette, I'm going out of my head.
It's awful! You act as if I'm dead."
—"Day, I'm exhausted. If you want me to deal
with all your bullshit, perhaps you should pay
for my fucking time." —"Don't be that way.
You know that I love you, and I know you feel
more for me than you like to let on.
I'm sort of your girlfriend. I'm not, like, a john."

—"You're not." She sits down. "But Day, you know how
it is. As soon as we talk, we fight.
Talking is useless. All it does is show how
we can't get on. I need some respite."
—"Okay, that's good." —"Day, just quit it!
It isn't good." —"But if we admit it,
then we can change it. I've got an idea.
What if I just move out of here?"
Bette starts, like she finds this notion surprising.
—"But where will you live?" —"Well I could go
back to my mom's" —"You can't! Just no!
That's not . . . it's so dehumanizing,
the way she treats you." —"I mean, it's fine."
—"It's not! She's nearly as bad as mine."

—"Aha! I knew you cared!" —"Whatever,
just because you're annoying as hell,
I don't, like, hate you or want to never
see you. I lo . . . I know you so well.
I just wish you'd fucking listen when I'm trying
to give you advice . . ." —"But I think that relying
on what you think is where I went wrong!
I wanted to be you, you seemed so strong
and clear, you know? Which I really desired.
But if I move out then I can pursue
plans of my own, like maybe do
an MFA, or maybe get hired
by some kind of non-profit. I have some ideas!"
—"These are terrible plans! They'll all end in tears."

—"Um, no they're not! You're so controlling!
That's why I need to get out of here!"
—"You've been talking about enrolling
in some college degree for like, a year,
and you're unemployed! How are you paying
the rent when you go? And if I'm staying
here, then how do I pay for this place?
I guess I can work at a faster pace . . ."
—"Well I could help . . ." —"No, Day, if you're going
you're going. It's fine. I guess it's a plan.
You can move out and I'll see if I can
make extra money. I might start hoeing."
—"But Bette . . ." —"I'm dumped. I get the point.
Now I need to work. Will you roll me a joint?"

She opens to her laptop, its screen blipping
brightly awake, and turns away,
and so do we, instantly skipping
to Queens, to my poor estaminet,
where I'm yet again (in a fit of folly)
attempting to cure Kate's melancholy.
—"Kate, come on, give yourself a break.
People do what they want. You can't, like, make
them not be dummies. You're not their mother."
—"I am their mother. I am, in a way."
—"Well then, I don't know what to say,
your kids are fighting with each other,
that's normal, you know? You let them fight."
—"Okay, I'm not their mother. Alright.

"It's just, I mean, then what am I doing?
I mean, I'm past my Saturn return.
I'm old. I spent my twenties pursuing
a career as writer, but I struggle to earn
a pitifully inadequate amount of money,
by selling listicles that aren't even funny.
I thought for sure by now I would
have written a novel, or done something good,
but I haven't. Being trans just devoured
my life, you know? It's like you lose
a decade. But at least I thought I could use
my knowledge to help. Like I might be empowered,
and wise and whatever. But I guess what you
are telling me now is that just isn't true."

—"Oh Kate, like, no, I think your writing
has connected with people, you know, a lot.
Like, Gaia likes it. These girls are fighting,
and that's on them, that's them, that's not
your fault . . ." —"But Gaia's the one who's acting
maybe the worst. I'm not even impacting
the people who like my work the most.
And my work is stupid! I was supposed
to do more than this! This . . . journalism."
—"It's not just Gaia! You're helpful to me.
Without you, I don't know how I'd be.
I know that sounds like narcissism . . ."
—"No, it's not, or like, that's fine,
you're allowed to have needs. But what about mine?

"I need to do some serious thinking.
And . . . maybe we need to take a break."
My face goes red. My heart is sinking
through my stomach. I start to shake.
Kate keeps speaking. "I'm sorry. Maintaining
a relationship is just so draining . . ."
—"But no, I love you, it's easy, we share
so much, and I need you!" —"Listen, I care
about you a lot, but perhaps I can't deal
with need. It isn't easy, it's tough,
actually. Nothing is ever enough."
—"It is!" —"It's not. I constantly feel
inadequate, as if I'm running uphill,
or like there's a hole I can't ever fill."

—"That isn't right. You really are giving
me things that I need!" —"And I can't anymore!
This is just surviving, it isn't living.
I think I thought that being your
girlfriend might stop me from feeling 'less than'
like I did with Aashvi, but I'm more of a mess than
ever! I failed at trying to be
cis, now I'm failing at being, like, me!
I'm failing at trans! I hate this relation
I'm stuck in to gender. Why can't I find
some way to get it out of my mind?
Some space for disidentification?
For holding it, and then moving on.
Imagine the freedom if your transness was gone . . ."

—"But freedom is immanent, not transcendent,
we're free within a scene of constraint."
—"Don't quote Butler. We're co-dependent."
—"Oh my god, I think I'm going to faint."
I run to the bathroom, and start splashing
water on my face. I feel like smashing
the mirror, the door, whatever's around.
What a fool I am. I thought I'd found
love, or something. Whatever we're calling
the state of not always being alone.
Idiot! Dummy! I should have known.
How at my age can I still be falling
for all this shit? Of course it's a lie.
—"I want," I say out loud, "to die."

But I don't. Clearly, given you're reading
this story I'm writing. You don't just die
from love. That's stupid. I do some pleading,
I beg, and argue, and even cry,
but it does no good. Kate won't be shaken.
And so she leaves, and I'm forsaken.
Did I mention it's cold? It's cold as sin.
I venture out and buy some gin,
several bottles, and a bunch of tonic,
and a number of packets of mac and cheese,
and I tell my boss I have a disease,
probably fatal, and pass the cyclonic
weather system, and my storm of regret,
by finding out how drunk I can get.

The answer, as it turns out, is very.
I drink for about three days straight,
and watch Survivor, and try to bury
all my emotions, love or hate,
or whatever else I might have going
on in my heart. Outside it starts snowing.
Fuck my feelings. I don't want to know.
The night comes on. It continues to snow.
The city looks like a crude engraving,
monochrome, simple. What a relief,
everything covered. But the night is brief,
and since the weather is now behaving
so strangely, I wake to a moderate day,
the enveloping snow just melting away.

Posted 12th March by @Eunuch_Onegin in series The Call-Out
content warnings: my mother
tags: forgiveness; foxes; knives; regrets

another year, another life?

(14/14)

New Year. Of course, I go out boozing.
Everyone knows that I'm a state,
that I'm fighting with myself and losing,
or being ground down by cruel fate.
A friend of mine has a shift bartending,
and asks me along, no doubt intending
to help. And yes, it's full, it's loud,
we know this by now, so yes, there's a crowd
of damaged outcasts, total messes,
frantically pursuing the desperate hope
that other people will help us cope;
our hair is dyed, we're wearing dresses
that don't quite fit us; we flap, we squawk:
it's us, the trans girls of New York!

I order a beer. Through the commotion
I make out Keiko, sitting alone
bent over a sketchpad with artistic devotion.
Nobody bumps her. It's like there's a zone
of calm and focus she's somehow projecting,
and even this raucous herd is respecting
her personal space. A subtle frown
crosses her face. She looks up, then down.
Her pencil moves, then her eraser.
She looks up again: someone's there,
a shining figure with fluorescent hair;
Keiko's aura doesn't seem to faze her;
the amazon speaks: —"Keiko? I'm Bette.
Day is my ex. I don't think we've met."

Keiko bristles —"Are you here to fight me
on that bitch's behalf? I don't want to hear
more white girl moaning. You all can bite me."
—"Not me. I try not to interfere
in fights I can't win. That's not my style.
Let's say that I'm here to reconcile,
or that I'm curious. I was also caught
up in that whole just really fraught
set of events you caused, or were part of . . ."
—"Gaia caused it! And Kate, and Day!"
—"Yeah no, that's not what I'm trying to say . . ."
—"I didn't want this. Right from the start of
this thing I was being pulled along.
Everything all of them did was wrong."

—"Yeah, everyone seemed to panic.
White women suck. I mean, speaking as one,
well, mostly, you know, my *abuela*'s Hispanic,
we're selfish, hysterical, and not even fun.
What can I tell you? You're right. We're dire."
—"Okay, so what, now I'm meant to admire
your self-awareness? Like you're the good
version of white trans womanhood?"
—"Think what you like. God, you're defensive.
Or maybe consider: is it possible you
might have done some things that were fucked up too?"
—"No, I'm the victim of very extensive
abusive behavior, and you want to judge . . ."
—"Relax. Don't worry. I'm not holding a grudge.

"But it seems to me like you have power
even if you prefer to keep it hid.
You're not at home like a shrinking flower,
you're here, you're watching, you're interested.
Every artist feeds on drama:
I think you'd get bored if your life was calmer.
And like, good news, this bunch of queers
output enough drama to last you for years."
—"Okay, well one, I don't have to be boring
in order to deserve to be treated right,
and I didn't like, force these people to fight
just in order to do some drawing.
I'm not insane. Okay, and two,
if that's what you think, what's the deal with you?"

—"What do you mean?" —"What are you pursuing?
Aren't you some kind of drama queen?
Or if you're not then what are you doing,
going outside?" —"I see what you mean.
Ha! *Touché*. So, what's my deal?
I'm not an artist, but I try to be real,
to know what I want. The deal with me
I'd say, what I value is clarity.
I can't stand hypocrites. I'm fine with liars,
but don't lie to yourself." —"And you dated Day?"
—"Well, she has clarity in her own way.
She's a dolt, but she follows her own desires.
She isn't pious. She doesn't pretend
not to will the means when she wills the end."

—"Whereas I do, is what you're implying?"
—"Nah, I like you. You seem kinda neat.
I'm just saying it's stupid to be denying
what community is. It's not nice, or sweet.
We mouth all this crap about communal healing,
but health is so dull. What we need is feeling.
Contact. Sensation." —"Okay, I respect
that you take a position. You aren't correct,
I think, or like, it's kind of simplistic . . ."
—"Not everything's complex. Some things are just clear.
Don't overthink them." —"I have an idea.
Could I maybe draw you? I have this artistic
project I'm planning, and I think you'd be great . . ."
—"Oh yeah, for sure! Let's make a date?"

—"No I mean, like now. Don't move your features,
but maybe turn your arms this way . . .
I'm doing these prints of mythical creatures
and you might be useful for the kitsune,
which is like, a fox impersonating
a person . . ." She starts delineating
a rapid, vulpine likeness of Bette,
and I look away and quickly forget
they even exist, because an appalling
thing has happened. There in the door
is Kate, of all people. I drop to the floor.
Why is she here? I begin crawling
around to the safety of the side of the bar,
to secretly spy on her from afar.

It's really Kate. She looks about her,
then moves towards the seat I left.
God, she's so close. Three weeks without her.
I want to touch her. I'm so bereft.
And then I realize that Aashvi is walking
along behind her. I can hear them talking.
Kate says, —"I think this is a bad idea.
I mean, I don't see her, but what if she's here?"
Like, what the fuck? Are they back together?
—"No, you must claim it. You need this space,
and you can't be shamefully hiding your face.
You think that I forced you into choosing whether
you could be with me, or else be here,
but they're not exclusive, as it seems you fear."

—"I know you're right. And I'm sorry I thought that."
—"Why would I try to force you to pick?
I always encourage you. I'm still distraught that
you think I'd pull such a dirty trick
on a person I love . . ." —"You're right, I was freaking
out, I'm sorry . . ." —"I know you're seeking
something important, at events like these,
but also you have to have boundaries.
You have to remember that they're resources:
take what you need and leave the rest.
This isn't a novel, you are not on a quest,
some band of sisters off on horses
to slay a dragon. You're an adult.
You perform an exchange, and produce a result."

—"But that sounds so cold. It's not a transaction."
—"Not coldness. It's kindness. If you know what you need
you don't have this drama, and all this extraction
of emotional labor. This emotional greed."
—"Can't you forgive me?" —"It's not a matter
of 'can I forgive?' I can't. When you shatter
a person's trust in the way that you did
the return of trust must be merited.
Which isn't to say it can't get better."
—"I'm sorry. I feel just swallowed with shame.
But what can I do? I was crazy. I blame
the testosterone. I know I don't get a
pass for that . . ." —"Oh Kate. Don't cry.
I want to forgive you. Can I say that I'll try?"

—"I need you to love me." —"Of course, I adore you,
although you've hurt me. Perhaps it's too late.
But look, I've come to this party for you."
—"It's true. You've taken me out on a date.
That's nice. I'm so glad this year has ended."
—"It didn't turn out as we intended
and it caused us both a lot of pain,
so perhaps we should toast to trying again?"
She pauses. "I still would like a baby,
and time is short. It was hard, I know,
but can we discuss another go?"
—"Oh god, well Aashvi, I mean, like, maybe.
But like, it's scary. It was really bad.
When I stopped my 'mones, I just went mad.

"But listen, I'm serious about showing
you that I've changed. I feel like shit,
but shit is useful when it comes to growing . . .
so maybe, perhaps, we can talk about it . . ."
and then they go silent. What am I missing?
I peep round the bar. Oh my god, they're kissing!
I know I should see the irony here:
the inevitability of this was clear.
The mythical character I most resemble
is Cassandra. I'm gifted with prophecy
but no-one listens, not even me.
I foresaw this all. I start to tremble.
I think what I'm facing is total defeat:
my humiliation is now complete.

Then I remember, there's another section
of this bar, downstairs. There's a way to escape!
I crawl through the crowd, avoiding detection,
though my skirt gets dirty, and also I scrape
my knees on some glass, accidentally tearing
my favorite tights. Flushed and swearing
under my breath, I find my way
into the basement, and there I find Day.
She's sitting alone. The room is deserted.
It's awkward. I smile and say —"Hello,
I guess this is where the cool kids go."
Day stares at me. She seems disconcerted.
—"What is . . . why are you saying hello?
You're supposed to shun me. Or don't you know?"

—"No," I say, "I guess I'd heard that.
Actually that meeting happened in my flat,
but you know, I think it's kind of absurd that
you just get banished at the drop of a hat
just on the word of some random committee.
Like whatever, you did some stuff that was shitty,
but it's not like I'm going to pretend you died."
—"Dead? I'm being crucified!
Last December I was so excited
about getting to go to a trans New Year.
Twelve months later, no-one wants me here."
—"Well yeah, but you must have been invited . . ."
—"Oh yeah, yeah I got the RSVP.
No! Who'd invite an outcast like me?"

—"Okay but wait, you're like, an unbidden
guest? Why not stay home instead?"
—"No, fuck that, I'm not staying hidden
away. If these cunts want to see me dead
I'll fucking haunt them. I'm not just quitting."
—"Okay, but then, like, why are you sitting
down here alone? You're not gonna scare
people who don't even know that you're there."
—"Well, I've also recently broken
up with my girlfriend, and she appeared,
and we're meant to be friends, but it was weird,
I kind of dumped her, and we haven't spoken . . ."
I start to laugh. "Oh, you as well?
Same with me. Do you think we're in hell?"

—"Oh probably, yeah." —"Here we are, competing
for resources, attention, or even 'likes',
with the same fifty people we keep on meeting,
everywhere, basically the other trans dykes,
who are also the only people we're dating,
and we're all so bad at communicating,
and we've all internalized so much shame,
and when we get hurt, of course we blame
each other, and our anger keeps on increasing,
we're all making lists of the bitches we hate
and if anyone suggests we de-escalate,
we can just accuse them of tone policing . . ."
—"Yeah, yeah, I agree with what you say."
—"Well so, why don't you just go away?"

—"Girl, you're talking like a coward!
The reason they hate me is because I'm strong,
and I'm not going to let a bunch of soured
joyless bitches convince me that's wrong.
No, I'll resist them. Like, it's my duty.
I have to stand up for the freedom and beauty
in trans women's bodies. Let them send
their messages to everyone who's still my friend
saying I leave a 'trail of predation.'
I know what they're doing. I'll show everyone
who's scared of this shit that they haven't won."
I pause to consider this declaration.
—"Cool," I say. "Do you think that there's
a way to leave without going upstairs?"

I leave through the back door. The illuminating
streetlamps obscure the stars in the sky
but reveal a woman, anxiously waiting
across the street. She turns, and says —"Hi!"
—"Gaia," I nod, admitting I've seen her.
—"Oh, I'm going by Proserpina.
I stopped being Gaia. Gaia, like, died.
So wait, can I ask, is Keiko inside?"
—"Yeah, she is, she's sketching and flirting."
—"How's she doing, does she seem okay?"
—"Yeah, I suppose." —"Then I guess I'll stay
out here. I mean, I can't risk hurting
Keiko again, like I did before.
I can't be that person I was anymore."

—"Wait, you're just gonna stand here? Really?
Why? And more to the point, for how long?"
—"If a Roman matron had been this sincerely
shamed, and convinced that she had done wrong
she wouldn't be home, in her bed, sleeping,
she'd be tearing her clothes and hair, and weeping
out in the street, or ending her life
either with hemlock or else with a knife."
—"Well yeah, but I mean, that's quite self-destructive.
Are you alright?" —"Oh yeah, I'm good.
I need to suffer. You know, I should.
This whole experience has been productive.
I think it's totally helping me grow.
Just leave me alone. Don't worry. Go."

And so I do. I make my exit.
All of these people are completely insane,
stuck in this cycle of builds it/wrecks it
endlessly reinscribing our pain:
our community, our precious gender.
I have to be tough. I can't be tender,
I have to put all of them out of my mind.
I do admit to looking behind
me once, at Gaia, poised in the distance.
She looks like she's waiting for a race to begin
and worse, like she thinks she's going to win.
Hope is the poison. Fuck this existence.
I text my mother: — "We need to talk.
Can you send me some money? I'm leaving New York."

THE END

epilogue: top-voted comment

50↑ 49↓
by @KateTheVampireSlayer

I'm one of the people whose life is narrated
in the OP's story, without our consent.
Because it's all weird and abbreviated
and has fucked-up opinions on what it all meant
I want to provide some context and closure.
Laura, who wrote it, lost her composure
(that's right, Laure, I'm posting your name!
You don't just get to pour out shame
on everyone else and not even mention
yourself. I won't let you hide underneath
an alias. The author is Laura Reith!
I know she secretly wants the attention.)
and disappeared. She didn't say
like, "Hey guys, I'm going," she just ran away.

So then super quickly, folks started freaking
out, and posting, like, "Is Laura dead?
Has anyone seen her?" Now, we weren't speaking
for reasons which you will know if you've read
her story, but still, of course, I was shattered.
This girl was my friend, my sister, she mattered
to me. I mean, I was really afraid.
And then it turned out we were all being played.
She wasn't in trouble, it was just that she'd ghosted.
She'd left her apartment, cancelled her cell,
but she was in England, alive and well.
Twelve months later she turned up and posted
this fic, I guess it took her a year to write:
the longest flounce post in the history of spite.

And anger is valid, and I'm totally aware of
the work of Dworkin and hooks and Lorde,
but listen, for real, it is also unfair of
Laura to make this grand and broad
critique of marginalized people trying
to support each other, basically denying
that solidarity is even possible at all,
by focusing in on something so small.
She's so involved in this personal vendetta
she refuses to pay attention to the good
in people, or just to our sisterhood.
I understand that what happened upset her,
and I'm not saying everything went well,
but there are sides to this story she just doesn't tell.

Listen, I also enjoy disaster
movies. *Dante's Peak* is dope.
But Pierce Brosnan running faster
than lava-dude, that inspires hope,
even if it tells us that hope is located
in the superpowers of an exaggerated
straight white hero, when really it lies
in community, and in social ties,
and in justice, the root of all resistance.
Call me a post-post-structuralist
but even if justice doesn't exist
we have to believe in its existence
if we want our communities to survive.
So what if the story was: we're still alive?

I personally know that we're all surviving.
Bette is still living at the same address
which means her business must be thriving.
Keiko is kind of an art-world success:
she was just in this swanky group exhibition
of new trans artists called "Phase Transition"
in Bushwick somewhere. Proserpina's dick
is conquering the internet in a porno flick
about Elagabalus. Day is still hated
widely, and still isn't making amends,
but even with her, at least she has friends:
her Twitter account's been validated.
Aashvi and I, I guess I should say,
are having a baby. She's due any day.

We can't believe it. We're both delighted.
And again, it sucks that Laura is sad,
and I'm sorry I wasn't more foresighted,
but it's not the case that everything's bad
just because we're no longer dating.
There's this idea circulating
that care is somehow a scarce resource,
especially for girls like us, and of course
half the world fucking hates us,
feminists, Christians, the government too,
but care's not a substance. It's an action we do.
I think that Laura underestimates us:
we survived the events she describes above.
We're all still here, still ready to love.

acknowledgments

For this misadventure's instigation
Jackie Ess deserves the blame.
The Golden Gate was my education.
My email list helped me write past my shame.
This became a book thanks to Jeanne and Cory.
Certain acquaintances served as a quarry.
I won't say who: I asked, they agreed.
Some generous friends were willing to read
various drafts, and their feedback was golden:
Melanie, Athena, Nivi, Ted,
Charles, Bishakh and Kaoru. Ed,
My agent, is awesome. I'm deeply beholden
to everyone at Seven Stories Press.
I owe Ali more than mere verse can express.

about the author

CAT FITZPATRICK is the editrix at LittlePuss Press, the director of Women's and Gender Studies at Rutgers University—Newark, and a noted society hostess, for a given definition of "society" and "hostess." She tweets @intermittentcat and main tains a website at catfitzpatrick.net. She is the author of a collection of poems, *Glamourpuss* (Topside Press, 2016) and co-edited the anthology *Meanwhile, Elsewhere: Science Fiction & Fantasy from Transgender Writers*, which won the ALA Stonewall Award for Literature. *The Call-Out* is her first novel.

about seven stories press

SEVEN STORIES PRESS is an independent book publisher based in New York City. We publish works of the imagination by such writers as Nelson Algren, Russell Banks, Octavia E. Butler, Ani DiFranco, Assia Djebar, Ariel Dorfman, Coco Fusco, Barry Gifford, Martha Long, Luis Negrón, Hwang Sok-yong, Lee Stringer, and Kurt Vonnegut, to name a few, together with political titles by voices of conscience, including Subhankar Banerjee, the Boston Women's Health Collective, Noam Chomsky, Angela Y. Davis, Human Rights Watch, Derrick Jensen, Ralph Nader, Loretta Napoleoni, Gary Null, Greg Palast, Project Censored, Barbara Seaman, Alice Walker, Gary Webb, and Howard Zinn, among many others. Seven Stories Press believes publishers have a special responsibility to defend free speech and human rights, and to celebrate the gifts of the human imagination, wherever we can. In 2012 we launched Triangle Square books for young readers with strong social justice and narrative components, telling personal stories of courage and commitment. For additional information, visit www.sevenstories.com.